"You leave, and the twins go with you," Finn said implacably.

"But I can't stay! I have a life."

"What life? What brought you to New York?"

"I'm going to get married," Izzy said.

Finn looked her up and down with such obvious disbelief that Izzy wanted to smack him. He smiled. "Have you picked a groom yet?"

"Yes, I've picked a groom. And I intend on seeing him this evening."

"You can't. Not yet. At least help me get the twins settled. Read them a story. Get them to bed." He was looking just a bit desperate!

We know you're going to love
FINN'S TWINS!
so much that we hope
you'll look out for the sequel,

FLETCHER'S BABY!,
in January 1998.
It's fun, emotional and will keep you hooked
till the very last page!

FROM HERE TO PATERNITY—romances that feature fantastic men who *eventually* make fabulous fathers. Some seek paternity, some have it thrust upon them; all will make it—whether they like it or not!

ANNE McALLISTER was born in California. She spent long lazy summers daydreaming on local beaches and studying surfers, swimmers and volleyball players in an effort to find the perfect hero. She finally did, not on the beach, but in a university library where she was working. She, her husband and their four children have since moved to the Midwest. She taught, copyedited, capped deodorant bottles and ghostwrote sermons before turning to her first love—writing romance fiction.

Books by Anne McAllister

ANNE McALLISTER

Finn's Twins!

Harlequin Books

TORONTO • NEW YORK • LONDON
AMSTERDAM • PARIS • SYDNEY • HAMBURG
STOCKHOLM • ATHENS • TOKYO • MILAN
MADRID • WARSAW • BUDAPEST • AUCKLAND

ISBN 0-373-11890-2

FINN'S TWINS!

First North American Publication 1997.

Copyright © 1996 by Barbara Schenck.

PROLOGUE

THE phone was ringing—had been for longer than he wanted to think.

Finn ignored it.

He stood motionless, his entire concentration focused on the developing tray where Angelina Fiorelli's lips were beginning to emerge.

He'd been waiting all day to do these enlargements, to see if he could find the perfect come-hither look in the best of the shots he'd taken the day before. He wasn't one of the world's most creative and eagerly sought-after commercial photographers for nothing. When he had an idea, he pursued it. And all the ringing phones in the world weren't going to interrupt him now.

He leaned closer and permitted himself a small smile as, in the dim red light of the darkroom, he made out the faintest hint of the luscious Fiorelli outline beginning to develop. *Yes!*

Another ring.

Finn gritted his teeth. Were the hell was Strong?

His matronly taskmaster of a studio manager shouldn't have any of his high-strung, ruffled-feathered clients left in the office to appease by this time. It was already after five o'clock. Why wasn't she answering it?

Angelina's famous pouting lips were now fully developed. Perhaps just a shade too sulky. Carefully Finn lifted the enlargement out of the solution and placed it in the stop bath, then submerged another.

The phone rang again—a half ring—then stopped. At last. Finn concentrated as the next set of lips materialized. There was a sharp rap on the darkroom door.

"Go away."

"Your sister's on the line."

He should have known. Meg had been calling him at inopportune moments since she was old enough to talk. "Tell her I'll call her back."

"I did. She needs to talk to you now."

"I'm busy. Tell her I'm busy."

There was a pause. "She's crying."

"Oh, hell." It took no imagination at all for his mind's eye to conjure up the vision of his younger sister Meg crying. He'd seen her—and heard her—often enough. Her sweet soft voice would quiver. Her freckled face would grow blotchy and her big blue eyes would swim with tears. Then she would hiccup as she tried to explain what latest crisis in her life had prompted her to call for help.

Finn knew the routine all too well. And Strong, alternately mother hen and Marine drill sergeant as the occasion demanded, was no better at turning Meg into a self-reliant human being than he was.

Finn sucked in a deep breath and snatched up the receiver. "Now what?"

"Oh, Finn!" came the breathless, teary quaver he'd expected. "It's Roger!" And the end of the world from the sound of it.

"Who's Roger?"

"Roger de Fontaine. You know! *Roger!*"

He didn't have a clue. "Some guy you've been seeing?" Always a good bet.

"The man I love, Finn." The teary voice wavered with an emotional vibrato. "Truly."

"Uh-huh." They'd been down this trail before. Plenty of times. Finn tucked the receiver between his ear and his shoulder and went back to contemplating Angelina Fiorelli's lips. This shot had possibilities, if only—

"If only I could convince him," Meg said mournfully.

"Huh?" Finn was distracted. He dragged his attention back to his sister, away from Angelina's mouth. "Convince him of what?"

"That I love him."

"Tell him." It seemed simple enough to him. He'd never fallen in love with anyone, so he'd never said the words. If he had, he would, not that he ever expected to. Why the hell did Meg have to complicate everything? Especially his life!

"I would, Finn, but—the girls are here."

"Of course they are. Where else would they be?" Her daughters, she meant. Twins. Red-haired, freckle-faced look-alikes with the unfortunate names of Tansy and Pansy—a product of Meg's airy-fairy period—they were five or six. Finn didn't know for sure; he'd never met them. He'd never met their father, either—another of Meg's true loves who had endured in her affections just long enough to impregnate her. The twins had been three before someone had bothered to tell Meg that he'd died windsurfing. Finn couldn't even remember his name. He wondered if Meg could.

She lived in San Francisco. He lived in New York.

She pestered him to come visit several times a year. "You could come out here on location sometime," she'd pointed out often enough.

He could have. He never did.

Keeping a continent between Meg and himself had always seemed the better part of good sense. And once she'd had her twin albatrosses, he'd found more reason to stay away. Finn didn't do children.

He didn't have to, he reasoned. He hadn't had any. Meg had, so she ought to be responsible. He'd told her so more than once.

"I know, I know," she said now. "But if Roger and I had a little time alone, everything would be fine. He's getting so impatient. We could get married and then they'd have two parents."

"Good idea."

"But I need to convince him."

"Hire a baby-sitter and go out for dinner."

"We need more than dinner, Finn. We need time. Days. Weeks."

"Weeks?"

"Only a couple," she said quickly. "Just for the two of us. But now that the girls are out of school it's harder than ever to get time alone."

"Send them to camp."

"Camp?" She sounded doubtful. "That costs a lot of money, doesn't it?"

"I wouldn't know."

"I suppose I could think about it—" the quaver was back "—but I do hate to ask Roger to pay for sending them before we've even..." She sighed. "And you know I can't." Meg lived hand-to-mouth, always had. The only times she ever got enough money to be even slightly ahead was when she talked Finn into providing it.

Like now.

Meg sniffled into the other end of the line. Finn ground his teeth. "You need to settle down, Meg," he told her. "Grow up. Be responsible."

She made a sound that was suspiciously like a sob. "I'm trying. I told you, Roger and I—"

"Just need time."

"Yes. He'll be a wonderful father, I know he will!" There was a little-girl eagerness in her voice now. "He's strong and masterful and so very smart."

"Good for him." Finn didn't say, then what does he see in you? Meg couldn't help it because she was vague and flighty.

"I'll send you a thousand," he told her. "You can surely find a good camp to stick them in for a couple of weeks for that."

"Oh, yes! Of course I can!" All the tears in her voice were gone. "I knew you'd help. You're the best, Finn. The best brother in the whole world!"

"Uh-huh," Finn said dryly. "You don't have to convince me. Convince Roger. Those daughters of yours need a strong, dependable father." God knew they needed one responsible parent. And Meg needed someone else to dump her problems on—besides him.

"I know," Meg said meekly. "You're absolutely right."

"So get them one." Finn hung up. Satisfied that he'd averted his baby sister's latest disaster, he went back to Angelina Fiorelli's luscious lips.

CHAPTER ONE

His studio—at least Izzy assumed it was his studio and not his apartment—was on the fourth floor of an old brick building in Chelsea. She found his name on the wall directory just inside the heavy glass door: FINN MACCAULEY, PHOTOGRAPHER, it said in small white letters.

"He's a wildlife photographer," Meg had told her, smiling, as she'd packed them out the door.

"Hmm," Izzy murmured now, glancing around, thinking that perhaps Meg had been misled. The fashion district was uptown, the Village was downtown. The city was all around. Horns blared, messengers whistled, brakes squealed, subway trains rumbled. There were buses, bikes, cars, cabs, and hundreds upon thousands of people everywhere she could see. No place for the buffalo to roam. And she'd be willing to bet there wasn't a deer or an antelope for miles.

But whatever Finn MacCauley had told his sister wasn't her problem. As soon as she'd done her duty, she'd be on her way to Sam's. Izzy squared her shoulders against the weight of her backpack, picked up both the duffel bags she'd just set down and headed toward the elevator at the end of the hall. "Come along, girls."

Two identical redheaded urchins fell in behind her.

"Is this it?" asked Tansy curiously as she gazed around the narrow, somewhat grimy-looking hallway. It smelled of stale tobacco smoke and other things Izzy didn't want to think about. "Does Uncle Finn live here?" Tansy persisted.

"Of course not. I'm sure he lives somewhere very nice," Izzy said with more conviction than she felt. She ushered the girls into the elevator and pressed the button for the fourth floor. The door rattled shut and the elevator lurched, then began to creak and rumble upward. "This must be where he takes his pictures. Of wildlife." Rats, perhaps. She would believe rats.

Eventually the elevator wheezed to a stop. The door hesitated, then slid open onto a tiny foyer with a door and a doorbell. *Ring for admittance,* ordered the sign tacked beside it.

Izzy rang. An answering buzz sounded. She pushed the door open.

He shot wildlife, all right. Just not the sort she'd imagined. Immediately inside the studio door Izzy came nose to belly button with a seven-foot-tall full-length black-and-white photo of a sultry blond bimbo clad only in her Rapunzel-length hair.

Izzy's eyes widened, then briefly shut in disbelief. She would have clapped her hands over the girls', but there were four eyes and only two of Izzy's hands.

"May I help you?"

Izzy's eyes flicked open. At the far end of the narrow reception room behind a desk sat a complete counterpoint to the bimbo. This woman was fifty if she was a day, with iron gray hair cut in no-nonsense bowl fashion, and dark brown eyes that seemed to widen a bit, too, behind tortoiseshell frames as she took in Izzy and her charges.

Izzy jerked the girls around so they would stop staring in openmouthed amazement at the photo. "I'm here to see Mr. MacCauley."

The woman looked doubtful, and Izzy didn't blame her. "You have...an appointment?"

"I've brought the girls."

The woman goggled, her gaze dropping to look at the twins. Her professional demeanor slipped suddenly. "Oh, my, no, dear. They have to be *much* older."

"They're six." Izzy started to argue. Then she realized that wasn't what the woman meant—which implied that Finn MacCauley was as irresponsible as his sister.

"They're not here to be photographed. These are his nieces."

"*Nieces?*" Now the woman's eyes were almost as round as her tortoiseshell frames. Her mouth pressed together in a disapproving frown. "You're...Meg?"

Whatever the woman's precise opinion of Finn's sister, it wasn't much better than Izzy's own. "I'm a neighbor."

"Whose neighbor?"

"Meg's. She lives next door to us. In San Francisco. We're not close friends or anything, Meg and I, I mean. The girls and I are," she added as she dropped a fond glance on them. They nodded their heads in agreement.

The woman looked dazed.

Izzy decided to press on. "But when they told Meg I was coming to New York to meet my fiancé, she...asked me to drop them off."

"Drop them...off?"

"At their uncle's," Izzy said firmly, in case there was any misunderstanding. "Mr. MacCauley."

"Oh dear." The woman contemplated the girls, then the phone. Finally she reached for it, then hesitated and pulled her hand back, apparently having second thoughts. "He's not going to like this," she muttered. "He's not going to like this one bit."

She reached for the phone again, but before she could punch in a number, the door behind her desk burst open. A wild man stalked out.

Izzy's stomach clenched. Her heart kicked over in her chest. He reminded her of nothing so much as the illustration she'd seen in a children's book her grandfather had once read her about a pirate.

A black-haired, clean-shaven pirate. His face was lean, all angles and planes. His nose was hawkish and had obviously once been on the wrong end of someone's fist or foot. He wore tattered blue jeans and a chambray shirt with the top three buttons undone and the sleeves rolled up. He was probably six feet tall, though he seemed bigger. His energy—or irritation—took up a lot of space. Meg would have said he had an aggressive aura. Izzy thought that didn't describe it by half. His straight hair was startlingly dark against the tan of his lean face and it looked as if he'd been raking his hands through it. As if to confirm her suspicions, he did so now, lifting it in spikes all over his head.

"Where are they?" he demanded. He stomped past the receptionist, then whirled and confronted her. "They're late!"

"I was just about to—"

"Call Tony. If he thinks I'm going to stand around here all afternoon twiddling my thumbs while his dollies drift in here when they damned well please, he's got another think coming!"

The receptionist started to nod.

"Now!" he barked. Then he shot past her back through the door, slamming it behind him.

"Was th-that—" Pansy began nervously, her hand strangling Izzy's.

"Shh," Izzy said.

The door burst open once more. The wild man snapped, "Tell him if they're not here in five minutes, he can damned well forget it. I'll shoot the next girls who come through the door."

Tansy and Pansy both gasped audibly.

And that was when he noticed them.

The girls tried to melt right behind Izzy's skirt. The pirate turned his stormy blue eyes on them. "Who the hell are you?" Then his gaze lifted to focus squarely on Izzy.

Izzy pressed her knees together to stop them knocking and raised her chin. "My name is Isobel Rule," she said firmly. "You are, I presume, Mr. MacCauley? I've brought your nieces."

She was past expecting that he'd welcome them with open arms. She at least hoped he'd say, "Oh, right, they were supposed to show up today, weren't they? I'd forgotten."

He looked poleaxed. "Brought my...nieces." He stared at the girls, his tan going oddly pale. "The hell you say."

Izzy frowned. "Language, Mr. MacCauley. Language."

He ignored her. His gaze narrowed as it settled on the children peeping out at him. "You're...Meg's kids?"

Izzy stared. "You don't know?"

"Never seem 'em before in my life," he said flatly. "What're they doing here?"

"I've brought them to stay with you."

The receptionist gasped.

The stormy look in Finn MacCauley's eyes increased to near gale force. "To stay? With *me?* You're joking."

"No, actually I'm not."

He didn't say anything for a moment. He shoved both hands through his hair again, spiking it further. Then, "Yeah, right," he said at last. He took a steadying breath and then gave her look of tolerant amusement. "So where's Meg? Hiding in the elevator waiting for me to flip out completely?" A corner of his mouth lifted.

"She's in Bora Bora," Izzy said.

All his amusement vanished in a flash. *"What?"*

Izzy took a step backward, almost toppling over when the twins' clinging made her lose her balance for a second. She steadied herself, cursing Meg for having stuck her in this mess. She shrugged helplessly. "She left last night with her fiancé. She said you'd encouraged her to go," she added accusingly.

"That conniving, sneaky, two-faced little—"

"Mis-ter MacCauley!" It wasn't all that far off Izzy's view of her ditzy neighbor, but she would never say so in front of the woman's daughters.

He bit off the rest of the sentence, jammed his fists into the pockets of his jeans and stormed around the receptionist's desk. She watched him warily from within the eye of the hurricane.

There was a sudden buzz from the doorbell. Automatically the receptionist responded. The door burst open and two chestnut-haired buxom bombshells in Day-Glo miniskirts trooped in.

"Oh, Finn, dear, sorry we're late! So much traffic coming down Seventh Avenue you just wouldn't believe!" the taller one said breathlessly.

They both brushed past Izzy and the twins as if they were pieces of furniture, skittering up to press kisses on Finn MacCauley's tan cheeks and ruffle his already ruffled hair with their long fingernails.

"Tony sends his love. He says thanks so much for the favor. Where do you want us?" The shorter one was already tugging her skimpy scoop-neck shirt over her head as she headed through the door Finn had emerged from. The taller one paused long enough to bat her lashes at him, then followed her friend.

No one moved in their wake. Then Finn rubbed a hand over his mussed hair in a vain attempt to comb it. He fixed the twins with a hard stare. "Sit there," he commanded, his gaze flicking from them to the bench alongside the seven-foot Rapunzel. They gulped audibly, then scurried to obey.

"You, too," he said to Izzy.

"I have to go," she objected. "I was only supposed to deliver—"

"Sit there and wait or take them with you."

Izzy's chin jutted. "I'm not taking—"

"Then you'll wait, damn you." Finn MacCauley's chin stuck out even farther. They glowered at each other. Izzy's glare turned decidedly mutinous.

"If you don't," Finn said, apparently no stranger to mutiny when he saw it, "I'll find you if I have to track you to the ends of the earth."

And he would, too, damn it, Finn thought savagely as he fumbled with one of the lights he was aiming at a pair of shapely almost bare backsides.

"Aren't you finished yet?" one of the girls whined. "I'm tired."

"You've been fiddling with those lights for hours," the other one complained. "It's late. Tony was expecting us at six."

"Tough." It hadn't been much over an hour. It just seemed like forever. Finn finished setting the light and stepped back. "Stop wriggling around, for heaven's sake."

"But it's hot."

"Tony never said it would take so long...or be so boring," the shorter one said grumpily. "The lights hurt my eyes."

"Too bad." Finn stamped back to the camera.

Tony's girls were still wriggling—and pouting. He sighed. He'd probably got as much work out of them as he was going to. He never would have used them at all, except he owed Tony a favor for talking Angelina

Fiorelli into spending an entire afternoon of her very busy New York jaunt in his studio. Of course it looked like the shots he took would end up being profitable for both of them, so Angelina was happy. But he still owed Tony, and shooting a couple of eager wannabes for a sunscreen ad that only required lots of honey-toned skin and absolutely no expression seemed an easy way to accomplish the payback. That was before he'd spent the last hour with them.

But they were preferable to what was waiting for him once he was done.

Damn Meg anyway! How could she have done this to him? What did she think he was going to do with a pair of five- (or were they six?) year-old girls while she went off blithely to Bora Bora?

It was patently clear what she thought—that he'd take care of them, just like he took care of everything else in her life. She had only to dump them on his doorstep and good old Finn would have no choice—he'd come leaping to the rescue once more.

He scowled fiercely through the lens. "Sucker," he muttered.

Both girls started. "I will not!" one exclaimed, jumping up and giving him an outraged glare. The other looked at him in consternation.

Finn straightened and raked a hand through his hair. "Oh, hell. We're done. Go on, get out of here."

They left, shooting him wary, worried glances over their shoulders as they went. Finn sorted and finished labeling the used rolls of film for Strong to send to the lab. Then he straightened the set, put away the pillows, moved the baffles, the lifts, the lights. Did whatever he could to delay the inevitable—the twins.

At least their minder was still there—this woman who'd brought disaster to his doorstep. He could hear

her even now. There were piping childish voices prat-
tling on while he wound up an extension cord, then Isobel
Rule's soft voice in reply.

She sounded mature enough, but she didn't look much
older than the twins. Maybe it was the clothes she was
wearing. They looked like she'd found them in a thrift
shop—or a dustbin. They were the sort of vaguely
dowdy, slightly hippyish togs that he'd thought went out
in the 70s.

She looked like some sort of out-of-work folk singer
with her long springy brown hair, parted in the middle,
and her fresh scrubbed face. She did have nice skin, rosy
with just a few freckles and otherwise absolutely flawless.
Probably too young to get zits yet, he thought grimly.
What the hell had Meg been thinking of sending the twins
with a child like her? What had Meg been thinking of
sending the twins at all?

And how dare the hippyish Isobel Rule look down her
freckled nose and chastise him for his language in front
of them?

It was mild compared to what he was thinking!

Maybe Strong would take them home with her until
he could figure out how to drag his sister and her presumably new fiancé back from their Polynesian paradise.

Yeah, that was it. Strong was a family woman. She
had a husband. At least he thought she did.

It didn't matter, Finn decided, making up his mind.
With his connections, it shouldn't take him longer than
a day or two to move enough heaven and earth to get
Meg back to face the music.

In the meantime, he could stick them with Strong.

She was gone.

"Where's Strong?" he demanded, glowering down at

Isobel Rule.

His receptionist was certainly nowhere in sight. In fact one of the little redheads was sitting in her chair—or had been until he'd opened the door. Then she'd taken one look at him and had scurried to duck behind Isobel Rule once more.

The apparently unflappable Isobel was sitting in a straightback chair next to the larger-than-life portrait he'd done of last year's supermodel, Tawnee Davis. It had graced the cover of the upstart glamour mag, *Hi Society*, and had won him industry acclaim for what he'd accomplished with Tawnee's lovely curves, a few shadowy angles and some artfully arranged blond hair.

Isobel Rule was a complete counterpoint. Rounded where Tawnee was curvy, covered where Tawnee was bare. Her curly brown hair not the least bit artful, her unlined eyes bespeaking innocence rather than seduction.

Not that she seemed to care. Her gaze met Finn's. "I sent her home."

"You...sent her home?"

"Well, it's after seven." She stood up and set aside the book she'd been reading. "The poor woman said she had been here since eight. She has a life—unlike you, apparently. So, I told her to go on. We all shouldn't have to suffer. She has to cook for Tom."

"Who's Tom?"

Isobel gave a long-suffering sigh. "Her husband." She shook her head. "Poor man, on his feet all day. I didn't know they still had beat policemen in New York City. I'm glad to know they do. It makes the city seem a much friendlier place." She looked at him brightly. "Don't you think?"

Finn's mouth opened and closed. He felt like a grouper, hooked, beached and gasping for air.

Strong's husband was called Tom? He was a policeman? He'd never known any of that. In fact all he'd learned about her in the seven years she'd worked for him was that she was never sick and she made things run smoothly in the studio even when the rest of the world was going to hell in a handbasket all around him.

He glanced around, trying to get his bearings. One of the twins was peering at him through the lens of a turn-of-the-century Kodak camera he kept on a shelf by the door. "Here now," he snapped. "Put that down."

This twin didn't seem nearly as skittish as the other one. She set the camera down, but she didn't dodge behind Isobel Rule's skirt. Instead she regarded him solemnly. "Why?"

"Because it isn't a plaything."

"I wasn't playing." Unblinking green eyes met his.

"What were you doing?"

"Framing ogres."

"Tansy!"

Finn's gaze flicked up at Isobel's dismayed exclamation. He saw a deep rose color suffuse her face, blotting out the freckles. And what a color it was.

"It's what you told me to do," the one who was presumably Tansy protested, looking indignant. "You said to iso—islo—"

"Isolate," Isobel supplied resignedly.

Tansy bobbed her head. "Uh-huh. Isolate scary things and they wouldn't be so scary anymore," she finished, slanting a glance in Finn's direction. "You're right."

He felt like baring his teeth at her. "Don't scare you anymore, huh?" he said to the child.

Tansy shook her head resolutely.

He turned his gaze on the twin peeping out from behind Isobel. "What about you? Are you scared?" He saw Tansy fix her sister with a hard look.

"N-no," the other one, obviously Pansy, replied.

"You ought to be."

"Mr. MacCauley!" Isobel's blush deepened. Or was it anger causing that color?

He turned a bland smile in her direction. "Yes?"

"Stop trying to frighten them! You should be ashamed of yourself, flaunting your ferocity before small children!"

"Flaunting my ferocity? Is that what I'm doing?"

Isobel Rule pressed her lips together. Then she turned to the children. "He's teasing," she told both girls firmly.

Finn frowned. "Now, wait a minute—"

"You were quite right to frame him, Tansy," Isobel went on, ignoring him. "You were clever to see that he's not really fierce at all."

"The hell I'm not!"

All three of them turned their gazes on him, the twins with jaws sagging, Isobel with her brows drawn down in obvious displeasure at his language. He scowled at her. But even as he pretended he didn't care, he felt the hot tide of embarrassment creeping up his neck and rued a complexion that, even tanned as it was, would allow Isobel Rule to see his blush.

He muttered under his breath and turned away. That was when he came face-to-face once more with Strong's empty chair and remembered he didn't have anyone to stick the twins with.

Except—and here his gaze slid sideways—Miss Isobel Rule.

Was she a miss? He looked a little harder, trying to see if she was wearing a ring, but she had her hands in the pockets of that circus tent he supposed she called a skirt. Their gazes met.

"Well, I can't keep them," Finn said abruptly.

"Meg said—"

"Not for the first time, Meg is wrong." He waved a hand around the studio foyer. "Do you see any dolls? Any blocks? Any puzzles or playthings? No, you don't. Why? Because this is not a day-care center. I repeat, not a day-care center! I can't take them." He did a quick lap around Strong's desk for emphasis, stopping square in front of it to face Isobel Rule and her two worried-looking charges. He didn't let his gaze linger on them.

"You're their uncle," Isobel said quietly. "They have no one else."

"They have you."

"Me?" she squeaked.

"Why not you? You brought them."

"Because I got shang—because Meg asked me to," she amended with a quick apprehensive glance at the girls.

Which meant that she was as much one of Meg's victims as he was. That, in ordinary circumstances, would have made him feel sympathetic toward her. In the present situation, he wasn't above taking whatever advantage he could get. "You should have said no."

"I thought you were expecting them."

He snorted. "You thought I agreed to baby-sit? You thought I said, sure, just drop 'em off, they can sit in the foyer and watch me shoot all day?"

"She said you shot wildlife," Isobel replied faintly.

Finn's hands tightened in a strangling motion. "She'll burn in hell—"

The girls gasped.

Isobel shot him a furious glare. "That's enough. Now you've terrified them. She's not going to burn any-where, girls," Isobel assured them. "She's fine. And you're going to be fine, too. Your uncle is simply upset. Obviously he isn't as flexible as one might like." Another accusing glare sailed in his direction. "That doesn't mean he doesn't love you and want you—" here she nailed him with a look that promised instant death if he contradicted her "—he just needs to get used to the change in his life."

"Our lives," Finn said, determined to salvage whatever he could of the mess she was making of his life.

A tiny frown line appeared between Isobel's dark brows. "What do you mean?"

"You want things fine? You want the girls calm and settled and reassured? Fair enough. But it isn't just my life that's changing. If they're mine for two weeks, they're yours, too, Isobel Rule."

CHAPTER TWO

SHE went with him.

Only because the twins—even Tansy who was by far the braver of the two—looked horrified at the slightest hint that she might abandon them to the questionable mercies of their uncle Finn. And because she felt morally obliged to make sure Finn MacCauley's bark really was worse than his bite.

And wasn't it nice someone involved had a moral or two? Izzy thought irritably as she hurried to keep up with him as he strode along Amsterdam Avenue.

Like his piratical forebears, Finn MacCauley had done considerably more barking and bossing on the way uptown. He'd snapped at the girls when they dawdled. He'd grumbled about having to herd them all into a taxi when the subway was so much faster and cheaper.

"Not with luggage," Izzy had argued. And then he'd groused about having to manhandle their bags in and out of the cab when he'd finally managed to flag one down. They had to disembark two blocks from his Upper West Side apartment because they were caught in a hopeless traffic jam, and now he was complaining about having to walk slow enough that six-year-old legs could keep up.

Izzy glanced around now, made sure the girls weren't looking, then kicked him in the shin.

"Sh—eee!" Finn hopped on one foot and bit off something she was sure would have singed childish ears. "What the hell—heck—are you doing?"

"Shutting you up." She gave him a saccharine smile. "How'm I doing?"

Finn looked nonplussed, then faintly guilty. He glanced back at the twins who were gawking at a boy on in-line skates weaving at breakneck speed through several lanes of still stalled traffic. "They aren't paying any attention," he muttered.

"They were. And you weren't making them feel welcome."

"They aren't."

She kicked him again.

"Ow! Damn it!" He bent to rub his shin and glowered at Izzy's sneakers. "Have you got steel-capped toes in those things?"

"Don't I wish," Izzy murmured. She fell into step beside him as he turned the corner and slowed his pace considerably. "I'm sure you're upset," she said, feeling a little guilty now herself at what she'd done. "But you don't have to take it out on the girls. It's not their fault their mother's a—" She cast about for a suitably polite word.

"Flake?" he supplied. "Ditz? Irresponsible idiot? Or would you like me to think of something stronger?"

Izzy tried to hide a smile. "Well, I wouldn't have put it quite that way, but..."

"I would," Finn said darkly.

Izzy knew the voice of experience when she heard it. "She doesn't mean to be quite so irresponsible. Meg is a dear, really," she offered. "Sweet, funny, eager..."

"Generous?" Finn suggested ironically.

This time Izzy couldn't suppress the smile. "In her way."

Finn snorted. He cut in front of her, bounding up the steps to a brownstone halfway up the block, then dropped the duffels on the stoop and fished a key out of his pocket. The twins pressed against either side of Izzy, watching him as he unlocked the door and held it open. ''Third floor,'' he told them. ''Forward march.''

His apartment, Izzy saw when he ushered them in, stretched from the front of the brownstone all the way to the back. Once she was sure it had been a warren of dark tiny rooms. Now it was one huge airy expanse with tall windows at the front and French doors opening onto a small terrace at the back. The kitchen area, on the street end, was small but efficient, with stark white cupboards and dark green tile countertops above which hung a rack with a row of well-used copper-bottomed pots and pans. In the center area, where they had come in, was a wide general living space with a gleaming hardwood floor accented by bold geometrical design, black and white area rugs and a huge modern black leather sofa and matching chairs and photos, not of seven-foot technicolor bimbos, but black-and-white studies of loons on a quiet lake, deer eating quietly in a clearing, and one lone wolf howling at the moon. Izzy stared, her attention caught.

''Move it or lose it, lady,'' Finn grumbled behind her and pushed her farther into the room with the duffel bags, then kicked the door shut. He dropped the bags and straightened, wincing dramatically.

''They weren't that heavy,'' Izzy said tartly. ''*I* carried them all the way through the airport.''

Finn muttered under his breath.

Izzy ignored him, continuing her perusal of his apartment, never having seen anything quite like it. She'd lived in the same San Francisco Victorian since she'd been orphaned and gone to live with her grandfather when she was seven. It had been cluttered and tumbled and homey. Nothing at all like this.

Against the corner provided by the back of some kitchen cabinets and nearly hidden by, heaven help her, a tree, she spied a steep wood and steel circular stairway ascending. At the terrace end of the room Izzy saw a warmer, more intimate arrangement of furniture with color this time—imagine that. There was a daybed, overstuffed chair, a bentwood rocker and several bookshelves—though it was clearly all high quality, not the mishmash of old and new, battered and worn, that still sat in her grandfather's house. Beyond the French doors, a terrace, with a small table and two chairs, overlooked the back gardens of the block. Not much, perhaps, but considerably more aesthetically pleasing than the row of dustbins she saw from her bedroom window every morning.

It was, all in all, quite out of Izzy's league.

"Finished gawking?" Finn asked. His arched brows mocked her.

Izzy felt her color deepen. "It's what you get when you invite bumpkins home with you."

Finn's deep blue eyes gave her a once-over, making her wish the floor would conveniently open and swallow her up. Then he turned to the girls. "You'll be sleeping upstairs," he said as he hoisted the duffel bags up once more. "Come on."

Izzy hung back until Finn turned, halfway up the stairs, to bark, "You, too. You're not sleeping down there."

"I'm not sleeping anywhere," she said. "I'm leaving. I—"

"You leave, they go with you," Finn said implacably. "I told you that."

"But I can't stay! I have a life."

"So did I." Past tense.

They stared at each other, neither speaking for a long moment. Then Finn asked, "What life? What brought you to New York?"

"I'm going to get married," Izzy said.

"You?" He looked her up and down with such obvious disbelief that Izzy wanted to smack him.

"Yes, me," she said flatly. "Want to make something of it?"

He smiled. "Have you picked a groom, yet?"

Which was what, his way of saying he didn't think any man in his right mind would marry a girl like her? Izzy ground her teeth. "Yes, I've picked a groom. And I intend seeing him yet this evening. So if you'll excuse me..."

Now it was Finn MacCauley's turn to grind his teeth. "You can't," he said. "Not yet," he added. "At least help me get them settled. Have dinner with us. Read them a story. Get them to bed." He was looking just a bit desperate.

Izzy chewed on her lower lip. She wanted to get to Sam's before it got too late in the evening. He wasn't even expecting her. She hadn't told him for sure what day she was coming. She'd wanted it to be a surprise. But she felt a certain obligation to the girls, too. Even if Finn MacCauley had been the best uncle in the world she'd have felt a little apprehensive about leaving them with a man she didn't know. And as much as she might like to discomfit a man as arrogant as Mr. Wildlife MacCauley, well... it was wrong to take her irritation out on the girls.

"Until they're in bed," she said.

Finn let out a pent-up breath. He looked at the two little girls who stared up at him in unblinking fascination. "Follow me," he told them and led the way up the curve of the stairs.

Izzy stared after him, heard him growl something at the girls, and hurried to join them. "Be kind," she said.

"Nobody's being kind to me." Finn pointed the girls toward one of the bedrooms. "Which of these bags is yours?"

"This small one. The big ones you're carrying are the girls'. I'll take mine back down."

She had just started down the steps when Tansy said, "Wow! Lookit this!"

All of a sudden Finn's hand reached out and snatched the little girl out of the room and shut the door abruptly. "In here," he said, steering her into the other bedroom as Izzy stared. "For now."

Izzy looked closely. Was that a flush deepening on Finn MacCauley's tanned cheeks? A smile quirked the corner of her mouth.

Finn dropped the girls' duffels in the smaller bedroom at the end of the hall. "Back downstairs," he commanded, herding them all in front of him. Izzy gave him an arch smile, which he determinedly ignored.

Once they were back downstairs, though, his battery seemed to run out. He stood and stared at them mutely, then looked at Izzy in silent appeal.

"Dinner?" she suggested. "You must be hungry, girls?"

Tansy and Pansy nodded.

Finn latched onto the suggestion like a drowning man tossed a life preserver. He headed toward the refrigerator with alacrity, opened the door, stooped and stared. And stared some more.

The girls edged over to stand next to him. Finally Tansy ventured, "You don't got much. Milk an' beer an' what's that?"

"Pickles." Finn straightened, sighed and shut the refrigerator door. He flicked Izzy what might have been an apologetic look. "I wasn't expecting company."

"How about take-out?"

Both girls jumped up and down. "Ooh, yeah!" Pansy exclaimed. "Moo goo gai pan! Kung Fu Pork and Beans!"

"Kung Fu *what*?" Finn gaped.

Izzy shrugged lamely. "There was this weird Chinese take-away down the street from us. Sort of...nontraditional." A grin flickered. "They specialized in dim sum and barbecue. Meg used to get supper there pretty often."

Finn didn't look surprised. "Whatever you say." He fetched a stack of take-out menus from a drawer in the kitchen and handed them to the girls. "Take your pick. I'll be right back."

While Izzy read the hard words to them, Finn disappeared back upstairs. Izzy was beginning to wonder if he'd vanished out the fire escape when at last she heard his footsteps clattering back down the wooden stair treads. She turned just in time to see him paste a smile on his face. "All right, let's get moving. Ready to go, girls?" he said briskly, heading toward the door.

Pansy shrank back, but Tansy came after him and thrust a bright pink paper menu into his hand. "This place."

Finn glanced at it. "Good choice." He opened the door. Tansy preceded him. Pansy hung back. Izzy didn't move at all. He looked back at her. "Well?" he said sharply.

"Are you sure you wouldn't rather have them to yourself for a few minutes?"

"Damn sure."

"Mister—"

"I know. I know. Don't swear. Come along. They're hungry. Who knows what six-year-old girls do when they're hungry?" He looked at them as if they might take a chunk out of his ankle at any moment. He made a growling sound deep in his throat.

Pansy, mistaking the tone for an indication that he just might take a bite out of her, skittered nervously past him. Tansy merely giggled. Izzy, seeing that he wasn't moving unless she did, sighed and brushed past him out the door.

The walk to and from the Chinese restaurant, though it was only three blocks away, was the final straw for two very tired little girls. The early morning trip to the airport, the long transcontinental flight, the taxi ride into Manhattan followed by their traumatic meeting with their uncle and another long ride uptown had done them in.

They barely touched the moo goo gai pan. They nibbled at the five-spice chicken wings, and they all but fell asleep in the bird's nest soup. It was a good thing the four of them carried all the food home to eat it, Izzy thought.

When Tansy's head dipped and jerked up, then dipped again and finally hit the table, Izzy said, "I think they've had it." Pansy had already been asleep in her chair for the past ten minutes.

Finn, who had been shoveling in food silently since they'd sat down, now said, "Thank God. Shall I carry them upstairs or will they wake up?"

The way he said it told her how much he wanted to avoid that. She wondered if he planned to spend the next two weeks ignoring them completely. He'd certainly done his best during dinner.

"I think you can carry them. Once they drift off, they're usually dead to the world."

"Had a lot of experience with them, have you?"

Izzy shrugged awkwardly. "They've stayed with us a few times." She stood up and carried her plate to the sink, then came back to pick up the girls' plates. Finn was still sitting at the table, watching her. She averted her gaze, focusing entirely on clearing the table.

Finally he shoved back his chair and went around the table to pick up Tansy. He looked awkward and more than a little tentative as he did so. When he straightened he looked at Izzy. "Come with me and pull back the covers."

Izzy followed him. Whatever Tansy had seen on the bedroom wall he had obviously removed while she and the twins were deciding on dinner. All she could see now was a king-size bed with a navy blue duvet, a teak dresser completely devoid of anything at all, and a couple of rather whiter-than-the-walls spots where two pictures had obviously hung.

He saw Izzy's glance go to the bare spots and gave her a steely look, then settled Tansy onto the bed. While Izzy turned down the covers on the other side, then brought in the girls' bags, he went back downstairs for her sister.

Izzy was just slipping Tansy into a thin cotton gown when he got back with Pansy cradled in his arms. He laid her on the far side of the bed, then stood silently by and watched while Izzy removed her shirt and shorts, then put a gown on her as well. Then she pulled the summer-weight duvet over them.

"Probably should have made sure they brushed their teeth," Izzy said as she bent to drop a kiss on each girl's forehead. "But I guess they'll survive one night without. Their toothbrushes are in their bags. I'm sure you won't have any trouble finding them." She flicked a reassuring smile in Finn's direction, then stepped back and waited for him to give them each a kiss as well.

He didn't move. He just stood in the doorway, looking down at the two small bodies in the very big bed. His expression was unreadable. Finally he sighed, raked a hand through his hair, and turned and walked away.

Izzy watched him go.

The girls wouldn't care that he hadn't kissed them. Probably Pansy would be relieved. But still...

It's not your business, Izzy told herself firmly as she shut out the light. *You did your part.* And that was true, but she wished she felt better about leaving the girls with him. She wished he had at least kissed them.

He was standing by the French doors staring out into the waning summer twilight when she came down the stairs. His hands were jammed into the front pockets of his faded jeans, his shoulders were slightly slumped. A swath of dark hair fell across his forehead. He didn't look particularly piratical now, unless he was a pirate whose ship had just been boarded and sunk.

Izzy would have liked to say something cheerful. She didn't think the words had been invented yet. She cleared her throat. "I...really do have to be going now."

He turned. "A rat abandoning the sinking ship?" he said, his mouth twisting wryly. The metaphor was so close to her own that she blinked.

"You'll be fine," she assured him.

He snorted. "Yeah, right. They look like they expect me to kill them."

"They're nervous. They'll calm down. It won't happen all at once. You can't expect it to. But you were a little...nicer over dinner."

"I didn't say anything at all over dinner."

"Which was a distinct improvement," Izzy said tartly. "But," she went on, determined to give him his due, "I understand what a shock this was for you. I had no idea Meg hadn't told you she was sending them."

"Yeah, well, that's Meg. A shock a minute."

"Surely you know someone who can keep an eye on them for you?"

He grimaced. "Strong. Though I don't think it really comes under the heading of office management."

"No," Izzy agreed. "Maybe she has a daughter." She paused. "But you wouldn't know that, would you?" He didn't seem to know anything else.

Finn shoved his hair back. "No, I wouldn't know that."

"It's only for two weeks. Take a vacation."

"Just like that? Drop everything and—"

She picked up her bag and began to rummage through it. "I almost forgot. Meg gave me a letter for you." She tugged out the slightly crumpled envelope. It had been slightly crumpled when Meg had given it to her, so she hadn't worried about simply stuffing it in her bag. Now she held it out to him. When he took it, she zipped up her bag and shouldered it, then moved toward the door.

Finn slit the envelope and began to read. He said a rude word. A very rude word. And then another.

Izzy's head snapped around. He was staring at the letter in his hand, then he crushed it in his fist. "She can't do this! Damn it! She can't! I won't let her!"

Izzy blinked, then realized that Meg must have used the letter to inform him that she was planning to marry Roger. "Maybe it won't be so bad. Marriage might be the making of them."

"Marriage?" He stared at her. "They're only six."

"I meant Meg. Isn't that— Didn't Meg tell you she was marrying Roger?"

"I wanted her to marry Roger!"

"You did? I can't imagine why," Izzy said with perhaps more bluntness than absolutely necessary.

"Neither can I now."

"Then what are you fussing about?"

"Because she's marrying Roger, all right, but she's decided she was wrong about him. He isn't stable enough or responsible enough for fatherhood." Once more his blue eyes bored into Izzy's and he waved the letter in her face. "She's given me permanent custody of the girls!"

It wasn't her fault.

Nor was it her responsibility. *They* weren't her responsibility. None of them. Not Tansy. Not Pansy. Not the black-haired pirate.

Going to Sam's was her responsibility. Seeing Sam. Being with her fiancé, beginning a real engagement together at last.

But she couldn't get Finn MacCauley and his nieces out of her mind. What would happen when the girls woke up? Would they have nightmares? Would Finn know how to deal with them if they did?

As the taxi whizzed through Central Park toward Sam's Upper East Side apartment, Izzy found herself worrying more and more.

It wasn't until the cab pulled up outside an elegant Fifth Avenue apartment building that Izzy let another worry enter her head.

Should she have told Sam she was coming?

Should she have called him? Should she have at least written?

But then, Sam appeared out of the blue on her doorstep often enough. He had never warned her. In fact every time he'd appeared in her life, he'd come unannounced, appeared on the doorstep, daisies in hand, a beguiling smile on his face, determined to whisk her away on some crazy, romantic outing. That was one of the things she loved about him.

Well, now it was her turn.

But as she peered out the window at the marble facade of the building, she began to have second thoughts. She'd never quite thought about where Sam lived until this moment. When Finn had led her into his brownstone, she'd thought it was the sort of place Sam might call home and she was pleased.

This building wasn't a brownstone. There didn't seem to be a multitude of brownstones on Fifth Avenue. Actually there didn't seem to be any. All the buildings seemed to be bigger and fancier, with exquisite wrought-iron gratings over tall windows, and heavy double doors set back beneath awnings. And they all seemed to have doormen.

Surely Sam didn't have a doorman!

But the driver said, "This is it, lady," and she knew, just as surely, that Sam did.

She fumbled in her purse for cab fare. Then, clutching her duffel bag against her chest, she climbed out. The cab sped away, leaving her standing on the curb, staring at the heavy oak and glass doors above which in gold numerals—maybe even gold leaf, Izzy thought with dismay—was the address to which she had sent all her letters to Sam.

Izzy ran her tongue over her lips. In all the time she'd envisioned Sam as her Prince Charming, she'd never ever thought he lived in anything remotely like a castle. *Why hadn't he told her?*

Because it hadn't mattered to him. *She* was what mattered to him—not the fact that he lived in splendor and she lived in a slightly seedy-looking old Victorian monstrosity that had far in the past seen more paint and better days.

She approached the doors hesitantly, two steps, then three, then stopped. She reached up and tried to judge just how messed up her hair was. Why hadn't she thought to comb it before she left Finn MacCauley's? She started to fish around in her bag for a comb when she was suddenly jostled aside as two very elegant young women swept past her, heading for the door.

Their hair was combed. In fact, not a single strand was out of place. Probably never had been. Izzy touched her own again, feeling the tangles and frizz. She bit down on her lip. They were wearing lipstick, too. She could see it as they turned to each other and smiled.

"It was gold. Sam saw it at Tiffany's. He told me so," she heard one of them say.

"No! Not really!" the other replied and gave a musical laugh. There was no other word for it—it was *musical*. And Tiffany's? Sam went to Tiffany's?

Then the door opened—not because they had deigned to lift a hand to do it but because the doorman—just as she'd feared—pushed it and held it open so they could enter. "Good evening, Miss Talbot, Miss Sutcliffe." He very nearly bowed.

Izzy goggled.

The door shut once more. But not before the doorman gave her a very hard stare. It was almost as if he'd looked at her and said, "Move along. Move along now. No riffraff here."

Izzy bristled. Doorman or no doorman, she wasn't turning tail and running now. Just because it wasn't exactly what she had expected, still it was where Sam lived. All she had to do was ask for Sam.

She marched up to the door.

It didn't open. The doorman just looked at her. She opened it herself. Halfway. And then the doorman grabbed the handle on the other side and held it there. "Yes?"

"I've come to see Sam Fletcher, please."

He looked down his nose at her, but he was too well bred to sniff. "Mr. Fletcher is away."

"Away? Where *away*?" God, why hadn't she called?

The doorman didn't reply. Discretion was probably his first name. And last and middle.

"For how long?" she asked.

Another dead end.

"Look," she said desperately, "I know he travels. I just didn't realize he'd be traveling now. We're...old friends." She didn't think for a minute Mr. Starched Shirt would believe she and Sam were engaged. "I'm from San Francisco. He stops by unannounced to see me when he comes through the city and—" She stopped abruptly, realizing what he might think about that!

Before he could remark a well-dressed—weren't they all? Izzy thought desperately—older woman came out of the elevator. She gave Izzy an inquisitive glance, then apparently decided that curiosity was rude and her gaze fixed on the doorman.

"Could you get me a taxi, Travers?"

"Yes, ma'am." He held the door for her, then kept holding it, obviously waiting for Izzy.

Reluctantly she followed. The doorman flagged a cab and held the door while his tenant got in. "Good evening, Mrs Fletcher," he said as the taxi pulled away. Then he turned and looked at Izzy.

"Mrs. *Fletcher*?"

He dipped his head. There was the barest hint of a supercilious smile on his face.

"A relative of Sam's?" Thank God she hadn't said they were engaged—even if it was true.

"His mother. May I get you a taxi?"

Izzy felt as if she had swallowed her duffel bag. She stared at her toes peeking out the ends of her sandals.

They suddenly seemed very bare. Very out of place in this world that was Sam's.

It occurred to her how little she knew about Sam. He was the grandson of her grandfather's beloved friend, the man whose life he had saved during World War II. They had corresponded for years. That was why Sam had looked Gordon Rule up on his way through San Francisco five years ago. He'd wanted to meet the man who'd saved his grandfather's life. "I owe him mine, in a manner of speaking," he'd said to Izzy.

It was the first of a dozen meetings—all at the end of business trips to the Far East—during which they'd fallen in love. So Izzy didn't know much about Sam's life in New York. She'd simply expected he lived much the same way she did.

It didn't take a genius to see how wrong she'd been.

Maybe it was just as well she hadn't found him at home, she thought now. She could imagine him being embarrassed if she showed up on his doorstep—no, in his marble foyer—unannounced. She didn't want to embarrass him. She was suddenly very worried.

"Miss?"

She glanced up to realize the doorman was still waiting for her answer. "No, um, thank you," she said faintly. "I'll walk."

Finn contemplated his liquor cabinet for a long time before he decided that booze wasn't going to solve his problem.

Only a fairy godmother who would wave her magic wand and turn his nieces into mice would solve his problem. Or one who would whisk them back to San Francisco and provide them with a stable, devoted mother who loved them.

He rubbed his hands down his face and slumped on the sofa. No, their mother loved them. He didn't doubt that. She had just finally come to terms with her limitations and, because she loved them, gave them to him.

He supposed there was a skewed sort of logic to her behavior.

I know you think they need stability, she had written in her letter to him. *I agree. And you must see that I'm not the one to give it to them. I've tried, God knows. But so far I don't even seem to have managed it for myself. I think I might be able to do it with Roger, but I don't want to give the girls hopes that I might destroy again. That's why I'm giving them to you. I know how you feel about being responsible. You never let me down. I know you won't let them down either. Thanks, big brother. I love you all. Meg.*

Quite a testimony.

How the hell was he ever going to live up to it?

He'd been too afraid of their unstable background to ever consider marriage himself. He hadn't wanted kids for precisely the same reason. And now Meg had dumped into his lap responsibilities he never would have chosen in a million years.

But she was right about one thing—she knew him—and she knew he'd bust himself trying to take care of them. If only he knew where to start.

The doorbell sounded, startling him. He glanced at his watch. It was after eleven. He frowned and hauled himself to his feet, then turned on the intercom.

"Who is it?"

"Izzy," the voice said. It was faint and slightly tremulous, and for a moment the name didn't register.

Then it did, and he pushed the button to unlock the door downstairs and jerked open his own door at the same time. Then he went out into the hallway to peer down as Isobel Rule made her way slowly up the stairs.

"What happened?" he demanded, looking her over, half certain she'd been mugged.

Then sanity reasserted itself. No one would mug someone who dressed like a thrift-shop reject.

She gave him a faint smile. "He wasn't home."

He dumped you? That and several equally uncomplimentary questions leapt into his head. He suppressed them, stepping back to usher her into the apartment. She stopped just inside the door and stood, still holding her duffel bag. He took it out of her hand. Earlier she probably would have fought him for possession of it. Now she let him take it. She looked as if she was about to cry.

Finn, used to the vicissitudes of emotions in the models he photographed daily, was no stranger to tears, although he was more than a little surprised to see the previously unflappable Isobel Rule coming close to them. "Tell me what happened," he said gruffly. He steered her into the kitchen and put the kettle on.

She sniffled and perched herself on one of the kitchen chairs, propping her elbows on the table. "He's gone— and I don't even know for how long. I should have let him know I was coming."

"You didn't?" He'd been reaching into the cupboard for mugs. Now he simply stared at her.

"He never told me!" Isobel protested. She sighed and ran her hands through her hair distractedly. "It's hard to explain," she mumbled.

"Try me." He was intrigued. Besides, it took his mind off his own problem.

"Sam Fletcher is the grandson of my grandfather's best friend. They fought together in the Second World War and my grandfather saved his grandfather's life. I used to hear stories about it when I was growing up. My grandfather raised me," she explained. "My parents died when I was seven and I went to live with him."

Finn set out the mugs and leaned against the counter, watching her, waiting for the water to boil.

"I met Sam when I was nineteen. He was twenty-four. His grandfather had just died and Sam was taking over a lot of the nitty-gritty work in their family import-export business."

"They own *Fletchers'*?" Finn's eyes widened. Fletchers' was one of the best-known import-export businesses in the country. While it might not have the household name recognition of a Tiffany's or Neiman-Marcus, in its own sphere it was legendary. People with incomes like Tawnee Davis bought their household furnishings and knickknacks from Fletchers'.

"You've heard of it?"

"I've heard of it."

"They must make a lot of money," Izzy said glumly.

"You could say that."

"I didn't know it," she said in a small voice. "I thought Sam wasn't any different than me."

"And he is," Finn guessed, beginning to get an inkling of what she must have unexpectedly walked into.

She looked morose. "He has a doorman. And a crystal chandelier. I wouldn't be surprised if it was Waterford."

"It is," Finn said.

Izzy looked at him, eyes wide. "How do you know?"

The kettle whistled and he poured water into the mugs for tea. "Because I shot a layout in his apartment building last year."

"You know where he lives?" Izzy considered that. "It's pretty fancy. It's very fancy," she corrected herself. "Sam never seemed fancy."

"Maybe he's not."

"You don't know him?"

"No." Finn hobnobbed with the recently rich and famous. The Fletchers had had money since they'd got off the *Mayflower*.

"I think I'm out of my league," Izzy said after a moment.

"But if he intends to marry you—"

"That's what he said. He gave me a ring." She flashed it briefly. It was a rock almost the size of a pea. "I thought it was a zircon," she said. "It must not be." She sounded even more miserable at that.

"Probably not." Finn thought she was the strangest girl he'd met in his life. Most of the women he knew would have killed for a diamond of that size. He shoved a cup of tea in front of her, hoping to forestall the tears he saw threatening.

Izzy wrapped her hands around the mug and stared into the steaming tea. "Thank you." She sipped it. "His mother looked at me like I had a social disease."

"*What?*"

She shrugged. "I didn't even know it was his mother at first. This lady came out while the doorman was rejecting me, and she gave me this look... it wasn't really snotty exactly, just aware, you know, like she was registering that I didn't belong."

"Maybe you're imagining things."

Izzy shook her head. "I don't think so." She sighed. "I don't think she has the faintest idea Sam and I are engaged."

"Not every guy tells his mother about the woman he's going to marry. Anyway," he said briskly, "he's a grown man. He doesn't need her permission."

"I just don't want to... embarrass him."

"You won't embar—" he started to say, then his voice faltered because there was just so far assurances could go, and assuring Isobel Rule that in her present state of slightly hippy shambles she wouldn't embarrass Sam Fletcher was too far.

Finn's eyes narrowed and he studied her closely, assessing point by point the woman he saw.

She wasn't tall and willowy like the models he shot every day. She didn't know the first thing about how to move with their sinuous grace. But she did have assets. Her shiny brown hair, if someone cut it and styled it and tamed all that riotous curl, might actually be lovely. Her skin was freckled, but not unattractive. In fact it had a sort of peachy-rosy glow that, if she wore the right colors, would be stunning. Slate blue, drab gray and burnt umber were not the right ones. A change of clothes would help, too. Something that didn't shriek Haight-Ashbury with an underlying hum of thrift-shop grab-bag for a start.

Her features were actually quite nice, not that she'd done the slightest thing to enhance them. She had wide brown eyes flecked with green and amber, a nice straight nose. And her mouth... he looked more closely. There was something almost akin to Angelina Fiorelli's about her mouth.

He could turn Isobel Rule into a woman who would knock all the Fletchers' socks off.

A slow smile spread across his face. "Izzy," he said, "have I got a deal for you."

CHAPTER THREE

"YOU want to make me over?" She echoed Finn MacCauley's words, trying to sound offended or at least indifferent. She didn't do a very good job.

He shrugged. "You're the one who just finished saying you didn't think you were playing in his league. I only offered to fix that."

"For a price," she reminded him.

"You scratch my back, I'll scratch yours. Besides, where are you going to go if you don't stay here?"

She didn't know. She knew actually that his offer was close to life-saving. At least it was face-saving. She couldn't imagine going home now and reporting to Pops and Digger and Hewey, the old sailors who shared the house Grandad had left her at his death two months before, that she couldn't get past Sam Fletcher's front door. They'd come storming out en masse and throw him overboard. They'd fuss and fume and get all over-protective and cosset and coddle her to within an inch of her life.

It had been all she could do to convince them she was capable of coming clear across the country alone to see him. If they'd known for a minute that she hadn't told him she was coming, well, it didn't bear thinking about!

No, she had to dig in and stay in New York. And Finn MacCauley's offer was clearly the best way to do it. All he wanted in exchange was that she take care of the girls. What sort of hardship was that? She enjoyed the girls.

So what was the problem?

The problem, Izzy finally got around to admitting to herself, was Finn MacCauley himself. She'd never met anyone like him in her life. Sam, who was apparently wealthy beyond all her wildest dreams, seemed somehow more ordinary, more commonplace, than Finn.

Sam was easygoing, casual, lighthearted. There was nothing intense about Sam—unless it was the romantic spark he had fired in Izzy five years before. Finn, on the other hand, positively radiated passionate energy. She'd seen it in him the moment he'd burst out of the door to his studio. She could see it now as he prowled the confines of his kitchen.

It was a sort of intense singularly masculine energy that made her more than a little nervous. She found that surprising when she thought about it, because heaven knew she'd been raised around men. Since the age of seven, she'd been raised *by* men—Grandad and his sailor pals. But not one of them had she been as aware of as she was Finn MacCauley.

Did she want such a man to, as he put it so very bluntly, "shape her up"?

Did she have a choice?

Well, yes. She could say no thank you to his deal. But then where would she stay? And who would he get to take care of Tansy and Pansy?

"For how long?" she asked warily.

"How long is Fletcher going to be gone?"

"I don't know." She didn't relay any more of the ignominious details of her encounter with the doorman.

"I'll find out tomorrow," Finn said.

He acted as if it would be no big deal. Probably for him it wouldn't be. No doubt she could learn a lot from him.

If she dared.

Visions of Pops and Digger and Hewey looking after her for the rest of her life—or theirs—rose again in her mind. She lifted her gaze and met his piratical one. "All right," she said. "I'll do it."

She was awake at first light, surprised, in fact, that she'd slept at all. But the previous day's events had been tiring enough so that it wasn't long after her head hit the pillow that Izzy was out like a light. The sounds of the city woke her again when it was scarcely dawn. She didn't know why sirens and rattling trash cans should sound different in New York than they did in San Francisco. She only knew that she was awakened very early.

She stayed in bed until almost seven, then went to check on the girls. They were asleep, curled in tiny balls in Finn's huge bed. Finn himself was bunking downstairs on the daybed.

"Unless you want to share yours with me," he'd said when she'd protested.

Her face had flamed. "I meant that I would sleep there," she told him.

"You need to be where you can hear the girls. God knows I wouldn't know what to do with them."

And so he'd left her upstairs in the small utilitarian bedroom that seemed to double as a home office. "Make yourself at home," he'd said dryly.

She had—more or less. Though she'd got a bit of a jolt when she opened the closet and discovered two large black-and-white female nude photographs leaning against the back wall.

"One guess where they were hanging," she'd said to herself, remembering the girls' gaping stares and Finn hustling them back out of his bedroom last night. She wondered now if he could make her look as sexy as those women.

What would Sam think if he did?

She was beginning to wonder if she really knew Sam at all. He'd always seemed like a regular guy to her. Her grandfather's best friend's grandson. No more, no less.

Now she felt nervous about calling his office and asking when he would be back. She felt nervous about seeing him again—which was crazy because she'd never been more comfortable with anyone than she'd been with Sam.

She brushed her teeth, took a quick shower, then dressed in a pair of baggy orange shorts and a faded red T-shirt, then went downstairs.

Finn was as sound asleep as his nieces had been, but not curled up. On the contrary. He was sprawled the length of the daybed, a thin sheet dragged across his waist, the only thing, Izzy suspected, covering a full display of blatant masculinity. Quickly she looked away.

Just as quickly, her eyes found their way back to him again.

It was, perhaps, an invasion of privacy. Certainly she should have gone back upstairs or at least into the kitchen area, ignoring him. She didn't. She couldn't. She looked her fill.

She'd seen plenty of semi-clothed men before. A girl didn't grow up in a house full of old sailors, even determinedly discreet ones, and not catch the occasional glimpse of masculine flesh. And she'd seen Sam in bathing trunks, shirtless. Not once had she ever been stopped in her tracks by the sight.

Finn MacCauley stopped her where she stood.

She remembered Tansy framing him yesterday, isolating what frightened her about him, looking at it closely so that it wouldn't be so scary. Izzy wished she could do the same. For in Finn MacCauley, even in repose, Izzy could see an elemental intensity. Even asleep he had energy. It was there, coiled within his lean hard body.

She'd imagined that a real wildlife photographer would have to be possessed of a wiry, sinewy strength simply to get out into the uncivilized regions of the world and take pictures. She'd never have guessed that a man who made his living photographing some of the most pampered people in the world would have the same strength. But it looked very much as if Finn did.

His shoulders were broad, his arms well-muscled. His stomach was flat and hard. His well-defined chest was lightly furred with black hair. It arrowed down past his navel, dipping below the sheet. Her eyes followed it. Her mind saw things her eyes could not. She blushed and dropped her sandal.

Finn muttered in his sleep, then shifted. The sheet slipped lower. He blinked, then opened his eyes.

Izzy averted hers at once and scrambled to retrieve her sandal. "S-sorry," she mumbled. "I didn't mean to wake you."

He frowned and reached up to push his tousled hair out of his eyes. "Wha' time is it?"

"Seven."

He groaned. "Do they always get up this early?"

"They aren't up yet. I...couldn't sleep."

He raised himself on one elbow. "What'd you have in mind?" His voice was low and seductive and Izzy found herself backing toward the stairs instinctively.

"Breakfast?" she said.

He rubbed a hand down his face. "Breakfast." The word was a low, despairing mutter. "Fine. You have breakfast. I'll sleep." And with that he rolled over and started to snore.

Izzy stared at him, amazed, wondering what he would do next. The answer came fairly promptly: nothing. He truly had fallen back asleep again. She stood watching him, tracing the line of his profile, thinking that he really did resemble that pirate in her grandfather's old book. And she was going to resemble the fool in another one of them if she didn't head toward the kitchen and concentrate on breakfast. If he had the fixings, she could make pancakes for the girls.

Surprisingly enough, he did. There was a box of pancake mix in one of the cupboards, and with the eggs and milk they'd brought home on the way back from the restaurant last night, she busied herself mixing up a bowl full of batter. She was just finishing it when a carrot-topped child appeared on the stairs.

"You're here!" The little girl's eyes widened and she broke in a grin.

Izzy put her finger to her lips, shushing her. The child looked guiltily and nervously in Finn's direction, then crept down the stairs and tiptoed toward the kitchen, obviously trying not to stir the sleeping beast.

"Are you hungry?" Izzy asked. It was Tansy, she could tell now that the little girl had come closer.

Tansy nodded. "How come you stayed? We thought you were leaving."

"I . . . had a change in plans."

"Good." The little girl smiled. "It's better that you marry him—" she shot a look over her shoulder at her uncle "—than Sam."

Izzy dropped an egg. "That's not what I mean. I didn't mean I was marrying your uncle instead! I meant that Sam isn't home just now so I'm going to stay here and help your uncle take care of you for a while. Until he finds someone else."

"Don't want no one else." Tansy's lower lip jutted out.

Izzy knew a losing argument when she saw one. "Go get dressed," she said. "And get Pansy up."

"She is up. She won't come down while he's here."

"She's going to get hungry then," Izzy said. "This is his home."

She had the first batch finished and was putting them on a plate for Tansy when the smell of breakfast cooking roused Finn. He sat up, letting the sheet fall away so that she saw, before she glanced away again, that he was wearing a pair of extremely brief underpants. He rubbed the back of his head with one hand and scratched his chest with the other.

"You really know how to torment a guy, don't you?" he mumbled, then hauled himself to his feet and staggered toward the stairs.

Tansy watched him go. "Mommy never said he was a grouch."

"He's adjusting," Izzy said. "I'm sure he'll be fine when he comes to terms with your being here."

"Doubt it," Tansy said frankly. She dug into the plate of pancakes Izzy put in front of her.

"You've got to try to get along, dear," she told the little girl.

Tansy looked at her with wide green eyes. "Why?"

"Because your mother would want you to."

"Why?"

"Because she knows you'll be happier if you do."

"Doubt that, too," Tansy said.

Another argument she wasn't going to win. Izzy sighed. Finn MacCauley was going to have his work cut out for him.

Now she heard a thump, a sudden harsh exclamation from Finn, a wail from the missing Pansy, a few of what sounded like placating words from Finn again, then further wailing and the slam of a door.

"Oh, dear," Izzy said as he came pounding down the stairs. He had on freshly laundered jeans and a pale blue shirt, which hung open, the shirt tails flapping. "What happened?" she asked.

He shoved a hand through still uncombed hair. "Damned if I know. I had to get some clothes out of my closet and I was trying to be quiet because it was dark in there and I thought she was still asleep. But she was coming back from the bathroom and I tripped over her. Didn't hurt her I don't think, but she howled and took off like a scared rabbit. Slammed the door on me. Damn near broke my foot." He grimaced as he wiggled his bare toes, then sat down to pull on a pair of socks. "She always like that?"

"No, of course not. Well," Izzy amended, "sometimes."

"Swell." Finn took the plate of freshly cooked pancakes out of her hand and poured syrup on them. Then he kicked out a chair, straddled it and dug in, eating wordlessly until the pile of pancakes was all gone. "Good," he said, wiping his mouth on a napkin. He looked at his niece. "Don't chew with your mouth open."

Tansy shut her mouth.

Finn gave her a curt nod of approval, then stood up and headed for the door, running a comb through his hair as he went. "Call you later."

"But—"

"Don't worry," he said over his shoulder. "I haven't forgotten. I'll have Sierra give you a call this afternoon."

The only Sierras Izzy knew were mountains.

"To set up a time to cut your hair."

"But—" Izzy clutched her tousled curls.

Finn flashed her a grin. "Have to start somewhere."

*   *   *

Cut her hair?

Izzy ran her fingers through her tangled brown hair, then crushed a handful of it against her scalp, savoring the weight of it, the thick luxuriant feel of it. She couldn't remember anyone besides her grandfather cutting her hair. Every first Saturday of the month he'd given everyone in the house a haircut whether they needed it or not. His clippers buzzed Pops and Digger and Hewey and whichever other old sailors were currently in residence. His scissors snipped off the ends of Izzy's increasingly lengthy mop.

"Shame to cut such a treasure," he'd always said, barely removing a fraction of an inch. So he never had. And now, with a blithe, "I'll have Sierra call you," Finn MacCauley was going to have Izzy sheared like a sheep.

To say she was having second thoughts was putting it mildly. To say she was having an anxiety attack was perhaps overstating things a bit. But not by much.

If she wasn't good enough for Sam the way she was, did she want him? she asked herself.

Was she overreacting, perhaps? Maybe his home would be far less intimidating in the daylight.

It was more. After breakfast she and the girls went to the park. "To explore," she explained to them. But somehow they ended up on the other side across the avenue from Sam's building. Its pale gray marble facade looked even more imposing in the clear light of day. It looked more solid, more substantial, more demanding even than it had the night before.

She knew she couldn't show up there unannounced with her unpainted toenails peeking out of her sandals and her windblown hair tangling down her back. Sam might be willing to take her the way she was, but didn't she want to be her best for him?

He was a wonderful man. She owed him that.

So, shortly after lunchtime when the phone rang and a cheery female voice said, "Hi, this is Sierra. Finn said to call," Izzy agreed to meet her at Finn's studio for a haircut.

It was, thank heaven, a day like any other—hectic, busy, by most people's account insane. To Finn it was the stuff of which his life was made: frantic stylists, demanding ad execs, fidgety models, temperamental makeup artists, slow-moving Gareth who helped set the lights and move the baffles. Other than calling in a favor from Sierra Jacobs and telling Strong to get him a list of nanny agencies when he got to the studio in the morning, he was able to put the Tansy and Pansy problem right out of his mind.

He worked flat out all day long—urging, soothing, cajoling, placating and incidentally shooting pictures. Getting eventually the look he wanted. And after he got it, he went on to the next project. And the next.

It was late afternoon by the time he got rid of the agency people, the stylists, the models, everyone—even Gareth. Then he disappeared into the darkroom and processed the film himself.

He didn't need to. He could have left it for Tabby and Alex to do in the morning. There was no rush, no need. Except for his own.

In the darkroom he could think about the film, about the negatives, about things he could control. Unlike his life. And the nieces he would be facing when he finally got brave enough to go home. And Isobel Rule. This was his kingdom. Here he was safe.

There was a sudden crash from the reception area, then a childish wail.

Finn groaned. His kingdom had been invaded.

Sure enough, when he stalked out, his prints barely finished a few minutes later, he saw one twin holding a dustpan while Strong wielded a broom. The other urchin was huddled in one of the chairs at the far end of the room. At the sight of him, she glanced around as if looking for somewhere to hide.

"Small accident," Strong said briskly, barely sparing him a look. "Here now, Tansy. Dump that in the trash can over there."

Tansy carried the dustpan over and dutifully dumped it. Then she looked at her uncle and lifted her chin. "It was an ugly ol' vase anyway."

Finn gaped at her, realizing what the crash had been. "You broke my Baccarat—"

"It was an accident," Strong said firmly. "She was showing me how to do the butterfly."

"Butterfly?"

"A swimming stroke," Strong enlightened him.

"There's no bloody water in here!"

"That was part of the problem."

Finn muttered under his breath, then fixed the girls with a hard stare. "What are you doing here? Where's Isobel?"

"In there," said the one called Tansy. She nodded her head toward the dressing room.

Pansy nodded, apparently unable to say a word.

"Somebody with purple fingers is cutting her hair," Tansy added solemnly.

Purple fingers? He knew that sometimes Sierra was given to flights of fancy when it came to makeup, but purple fingers? He looked at Strong for confirmation.

She nodded, then handed him a sheet of paper. "Here's the list of agencies with possible nannies."

"Nannies?" Tansy latched onto the word at once. She looked at him worriedly. "Like Mary Poppins?"

"Maybe that dog in *Peter Pan*," her twin suggested in a voice barely loud enough for Finn to hear. "Nana."

Tansy's eyes widened. "Oooh, yes." Her eyes shone and she looked at Finn. "Are we gonna get a dog?"

"No, we're not going to get a dog!"

Both girls' faces fell. They looked at him pitifully.

Finn raked his fingers through his hair in desperation. "You can't have a dog in the city. It's not fair to the dog."

Neither girl said a word. They just continued to look. He glanced at Strong, hoping for support. "You don't have a dog, do you?"

She gave Finn an apologetic smile. "Two of them. Golden retrievers."

"Do they got puppies?" Tansy asked eagerly.

"No," she said.

Thank God, Finn thought. "Forget dogs," he said firmly just as the door to the dressing room opened and Isobel came in.

He stared at her, stunned. Where once all he had seen was a mop of unruly brown hair, now he saw a face— an astonishingly pretty face, with high cheekbones, a small straight nose and a pair of lips that would definitely give Angelina Fiorelli a run for her money. And the face was framed, accentuated, by a swingy layered cut that lay easily against her head. It moved as she did, lightly, effortlessly.

"Not bad, huh?" Sierra said, waggling purple fingers at him. Her own spiky short hair was purple, too, which probably accounted for the fingers, but no one seemed to consider that worthy of mention.

Izzy gave him a tentative, somewhat nervous smile.

Finn ran his tongue over dry lips. "Not bad," he agreed finally. *Not bad at all.* Who the hell would have thought it? He shook his head.

That apparently made Izzy even more nervous. "Really?"

"'s beautiful," Tansy told her, and Pansy nodded, eyes wide. Her hand went to her own hair, twisting a lock around her fingers.

Sierra grinned. "Want me to do them, too?" she asked Finn.

Before he could open his mouth to get out an answer one way or the other, Tansy beamed. "Yes!" and skipped past them all into the dressing room.

Finn looked at Izzy for approval. She shrugged.

"Go for it," he said to Sierra. "Maybe you could give one a haircut and not the other. Then I could tell them apart."

Izzy frowned. "You need to be able to tell them apart without haircuts to help you."

"I need time for that," Finn said.

"You'll have plenty."

Exactly what he was afraid of. His glower made Pansy edge behind Strong's chair.

"Izzy," Tansy called from the dressing room. "Come watch!"

Izzy went and Pansy, crablike, skittered after her.

Finn stood where he was, hands shoved into the pockets of his jeans, and watched them all. Then he slipped back into his studio and picked up his camera and returned, still staying outside the room, shooting picture after picture as Izzy and Sierra, Tansy and even Pansy, oblivious to him, discussed how Tansy's hair should be cut.

As Sierra snipped, the mass of coppery ringlets gave way to a pixieish halo that framed the little girl's face. And Tansy's expression went from nervousness to amazement to enthusiasm.

Finn, shooting into the mirror, caught it all—Sierra's intense concentration, Pansy's interest, Izzy's delight. He caught Izzy running her fingers through Tansy's short hair, fluffing it and smiling. He caught Tansy holding a fluffy ball of her own recently shorn hair. He caught Pansy scrambling into the chair as soon as Tansy got out of it. He shot Izzy and Tansy and Pansy, all three of them, beaming at Sierra when she had finished. He shot Sierra giving them a purple-fingered victory sign.

He didn't have to print the film to know it was good. He had a story, had framed a slice of life. His nieces' life. Once again their kinship was born in on him. They seemed less strangers and more a part of him. He wondered that their mother had been so ready to give them up. Wasn't sharing these two little girls' lives worth some kind of effort?

Izzy seemed to think so. At least she was sharing it now.

Maybe Meg couldn't. Just like their mother and father hadn't. Finn's jaw tightened.

Just then Izzy looked over at him and smiled. It was a sweet, gentle smile—almost a comforting smile, as if she knew somehow what he was feeling.

Did she know? *How* did she know?

And how could a simple haircut make her so damn beautiful?

Izzy loved her haircut. All evening and all the next day she kept reaching up to run her fingers through it, ruffling it and shaking her head to make it swing, conscious always of how light her head felt—as if someone had removed the anchor weighing her down.

She whistled a tentative phrase of "Anchors Aweigh" and snickered at her own idiocy. But she couldn't stop touching it—or glancing at it in every mirror or shop window she passed. And whenever she glimpsed her reflection, she tossed her head to watch her hair swing out and fall back into perfect place.

"People will think you have a tic," she admonished herself.

"Who you talkin' to?" Tansy asked her.

They were walking over to the park late in the afternoon, passing a shop with skulls and bones and brass incense holders in the window, and she was busy fluffing out her hair. She felt her face warm and she gave Tansy a guilty look. "No one."

"Your hair's pretty," Pansy told her.

Izzy turned her self-conscious smile on Pansy. "Thanks. So's yours."

"I like Sierra," Tansy said. "D'you suppose I could have purple hair, Izzy?"

"No, my dear, you could not," said a voice behind them, and Izzy jerked around to see Finn, camera bag slung over his shoulder, coming up the sidewalk.

The look he gave Tansy had her stepping backward worriedly. But then his lips quirked and he reached out a hand and ruffled it through her coppery curls. "I like it just the way it is."

She blinked, then gave him a faint, tentative smile.

"Where did you come from?" Izzy asked him.

He wiped a hand through sweat-dampened dark hair and jerked his head. "Up from the subway."

"You're finished early."

"Some days I get done earlier than others." He sounded almost defensive. It surprised her.

"We were going to get an ice cream and then walk by the lake. Want to join us?" *Say yes,* she implored him silently. Not because she wanted him to, but because he needed to make connections with the girls.

Finn hesitated. "Yeah, all right. I guess I could. An ice cream sounds pretty good right now." He shifted his camera bag to his other shoulder and fell into step beside them.

Behind his back the girls glowered at her. Izzy gave them a bright smile, deliberately ignoring their silent protest. She knew he made them uncomfortable, but nothing was going to change that but getting to know him better. She wondered if he had deliberately quit early today in an effort to spend some time with them. Would he admit it if she asked?

As they entered the park, Tansy skipped on ahead. Pansy lagged behind, then seemed to notice that doing so allowed Finn to walk almost on her heels. She sped up, catching her sister. Izzy was left to walk with Finn alone. Neither of them spoke.

Finally Izzy ventured, "It was . . . nice of you to come home early."

"I was done."

"You could have hung around developing film or something."

"D'you wish I had?" There was a brusque challenge in his voice.

"No, of course not."

But he shoved his hands into his pockets and scuffed along and Izzy wondered if she'd offended him. What was underneath the gruff exterior he showed to the world? As she watched him out of the corner of her eye, he kept his eyes on the girls. He was watching them like they were an unknown species. Izzy was beginning to suppose they were.

"You don't photograph children often, do you?" she asked.

"Not very."

"Don't you like to?"

He shrugged. "Never thought about it. It isn't what they pay me for." He kicked at a fallen branch in what looked to her now like determined disinterest. She liked watching him. Much more used to the elderly men with whom she had lived, she wasn't accustomed to the easy grace of a man in his prime. Of course there was Sam—but she saw Sam so briefly and at such sporadic intervals that she was always busy listening to him, being enchanted by him. She'd never paid any attention to the way he moved.

"What're you staring at?" Finn demanded now.

Izzy jerked her gaze away. "Nothing," she said quickly. "Just...thought I saw a bird over there." She doubted he believed her, but at least he didn't ask her any further questions. And the girls had reached the ice cream vendor now, so she was saved from having to come up with anything else.

Finn bought them all ice creams. He ate his own quickly, not savoring it—or spilling it—like the girls did. And as soon as he finished, Izzy saw him open his camera bag and take out a small camera. He pointed it at her. She stuck her ice-cream-covered tongue out at him. He shot the picture.

"Oh, you!"

He grinned unrepentantly. "Saving your haircut for posterity."

Izzy's hand immediately flew to her hair to smooth it. It was already smooth.

"It's fine," Finn told her as he snapped another—and another. Then he turned the camera on the girls. They weren't nearly as self-conscious as Izzy was. They mugged and preened—particularly, of course, Tansy—and dribbled ice cream down their chins with a complete lack of concern. At least *they* didn't stick their tongues out at him.

Finally they simply ignored him, grabbing Izzy's hands with sticky ones of their own and dragging her toward the boat house. She noticed that Finn followed, keeping a distance, watching, occasionally shooting another picture or two.

Izzy rented a boat. She and the girls clambered in. She looked over at Finn and motioned for him to come. "There's plenty of room."

He shook his head. "Go on. I'm fine."

Izzy started to protest, but the girls urged, "Come on, Izzy. Let's go!" So finally she shrugged and fitted the oars into the locks and had Tansy shove them away from the dock. She'd learned to row at an early age. Her grandfather had considered it a necessary accomplishment. Reading, writing, 'rithmetic, riding and rowing were equally important to Gordon Rule. Though they had mostly sailed whenever he had taken her out on the bay, she was glad now to have spent all those hours rowing. At least she didn't feel like an incompetent while Finn walked around the shore of the lake snapping pictures of them.

She even gave each of the girls a turn. They were small and the oars were big and hard to maneuver, but she figured they could each get a start. Tansy, in her enthusiasm, almost knocked Izzy's head off with one, and Pansy nearly lost one in the water. But they tried hard, and they laughed a lot and Izzy laughed, too, and every once in a while she would glance over at Finn on the bank and wish he had come along so he could really get to know these lovely little girls.

When their time was up, he was waiting on the dock when they climbed out.

"Did you see me row?" Tansy asked him, her bright eyes shining.

"You did good."

Tansy agreed. "For my first time," she said matter-of-factly. "I'd rather swim, but it was fun. What'll we do now?" she asked Izzy.

Izzy said, "I think it's about time to go back to the apartment and start fixing supper."

Finn fell in alongside her. "When did you learn to row?"

Izzy hadn't said too much about her grandfather or her background. Now she found herself telling him about life with the loving and completely unconventional man who had raised her.

"He'd had one son who, because he'd been in the Navy and then in the merchant marine, was mostly raised by his wife. He didn't know anything about raising children—especially little girls—but he just dug in and made up his mind to do it." Her eyes got a faraway look in them as she remembered so many of the things they'd done. "I learned a lot of things most little girls never do." She looked up at Finn and smiled. "We learned together."

"Is this a pep talk?" he asked suspiciously.

"Let's just say that my grandfather did a very good job and I wouldn't have missed a minute of it. I think you can, too."

CHAPTER FOUR

FINN suspected that Izzy's grandfather, notwithstanding his many years at sea, had had a lot more experience being a part of a loving, responsible family than Finn did.

All Finn had were a few memories that were so early and so fleeting that sometimes he wondered if he hadn't simply imagined them, and nine years of being jerked from one foster home to another—some better, some worse—but always someone else's home. Never his.

He couldn't remember ever feeling like he belonged somewhere. He didn't know how to relax, let down his guard, open his heart. Hell, sometimes he thought he didn't have a heart. And he wasn't entirely sorry. Hearts got broken. His had been so many years ago that whatever he had left only beat. It didn't love. He didn't know how.

Izzy did. It didn't take him long to discover that.

He watched her when she was with the girls, smiling, teasing, playing, reading them a book, showing them how to slice carrots, teaching them how to row. He watched when she smoothed their curls away from their faces, when she gave their hands an extra squeeze, when she bowed her head and said their prayers with them, when she bent to kiss them good-night.

Sometimes his throat hurt when he watched. He wondered if he was coming down with a cold, but it was a damned selective virus. It only flared up around Izzy. He took refuge behind his camera lens. It beat tissue, and he got all the kisses, all the smiles, all the gentle touches down on film.

He didn't dare try them himself.

Tansy spoke to him now and then—but only if she was so caught up in the moment that she forgot who he was. When she remembered, she retreated. He remembered having done that, remembered thinking, what if he started to like someone, to trust someone—and they left? What if he was wrong to trust? What if they weren't trustworthy at all?

A part of him wanted to warn them against trusting Izzy. She was going to leave them, after all. She was only waiting until her beloved Sam returned.

He was due back in the middle of the following week. Finn had found that out by calling his office. Then Izzy called and left a message, telling him she was in town and leaving the number at Finn's place. So really it was only a matter of time.

And knowing that annoyed him. But when he challenged her about it one night after she'd got the girls tucked up in bed and had come back downstairs, she had looked totally surprised.

"What do you mean, won't I be betraying them?"

"You're going to leave!" he pointed out. "Hell, you'd be gone now if your boyfriend had been there to take you in!"

"I would have come and visited. I would have had them over to see me. I wasn't going to walk out of their lives."

"Yeah?" he said doubtfully.

"Yeah," Izzy replied in exactly the same truculent tone. Then she smiled at him, a sweet smile. An angel's smile. "I would never abandon a friend, Finn."

And, God help him, he believed her.

But just the same, he intended to make damn sure that she stayed around for the girls as long as they needed her. So during the next week—a week in which Isobel took his list and dutifully lined up half a dozen interviews for prospective nannies—he prepared to find something wrong with all of them. As it happened, one by one they all got shot down.

And the true beauty of it was that Finn didn't have to do any of the shooting. Tansy and Pansy and, once, even Isobel herself, took care of that.

One was "too grouchy," one was "too neat." One "didn't have any sense of humor," another "didn't seem very clean." One was "too slow," and the last "had a pierced nose and some rather risqué tattoos."

"Wish I'd seen her," Finn said, grinning when Izzy told him.

It was Thursday night. They'd—no, *she'd*—got the girls to bed and now they were sitting in the living area, he at one end of the black leather sofa, Isobel and all her interviewing notes at the other. She had her legs curled under her, and he still thought she looked like a bird in a nest, sort of fluffy and appealing. Her new haircut seemed a part of her now, highlighting her bright, expressive face, making her extremely appealing. It was shaggy and seemed to move and bounce when she did. His fingers itched to touch it, to ruffle her feathers. He knew he was supposed to be commiserating with her efforts, but he didn't much feel like it. He felt more like shoving her notes and scribblings on the floor and spending the time in a more interesting way.

He shoved the thought away. She was engaged to Sam Fletcher, for God's sake!

Isobel, completely unaware of the direction of his thoughts, laughed. "She was a classic, that girl. I'm used to a far-out types. San Francisco has its share. But this one—'' she shook her head ''—she'd have given the girls an education.''

Finn didn't think they needed an education. He was out of his league dealing with his nieces just the way they were. Not that he spent much time trying. They still intimidated him. And they hadn't exactly been eager for his company, either.

''—don't know where we're going to come up with any more candidates,'' Isobel was saying.

''What's the hurry?''

''I've been here a week!''

''Sam's still gone. And we haven't finished making you over yet.''

Izzy touched her hair self-consciously. ''I'm...all right,'' she said. ''Feeling braver.''

''Good. But if you think Amelia Fletcher is going to ooh and aah over those wretched plaid shorts you're wearing...''

Izzy flushed and squirmed in her corner of the sofa. ''They're comfortable. Maybe you're right. Maybe I should get some better clothes.''

''Different clothes. I have a friend who will help you.''

''But—''

''It's part of the deal,'' he said firmly. ''So's the manicure you're getting tomorrow morning.'' He reached over and picked up one of her hands. Her nails were a far cry from the clean smooth ovals of the women he saw every day.

''Picture framer's nails,'' she said now and tugged her hand away from his, hiding the torn cuticles and rough-edged nails beneath the hem of her shirt. ''It's an occupational hazard.''

''Think Sam will allow it?'' He saw her fingers tighten into fists and felt guilty for preying on her insecurities.

"Don't worry about it. Just show up. Carlota is doing me a special favor."

Izzy folded her arms across her chest. "I don't need special favors."

"Stubborn, are we?" he mocked her. "That's impressive. And so mature. She's coming all the way in from Bayside."

Izzy pressed her lips together, then sagged slightly. "Oh, all right."

Finn gave a satisfied nod. Izzy sighed and stretched her arms over her head. On one of his models Finn would have been able to catch a glimpse of an inch or two of bare midriff. On Izzy all he got was a voluminous amount of chartreuse T-shirt.

Still he found himself watching her more than he liked. She might not have the grace of his models, but she moved easily, artlessly. Used as he was to women who did everything with such calculation, it was a pleasure to watch Izzy simply move with enthusiasm, with joy.

He didn't only watch her move. He watched the way she acted. He liked seeing her by herself. He liked seeing her with the girls.

When he was a kid, he remembered having fantasies about what a mother ought to be like. He didn't much remember his own, and what he did remember wasn't the stuff of which fantasies were made. But the feelings he got watching Izzy with the girls recalled those fantasies.

Next thing you know you'll want her in there tucking you in at night, too, he thought wryly. *Only if she gets in, too,* was the thought immediately following.

As if she'd read his mind, Izzy bounced up off the sofa. "Well," she said briskly, "it's getting late. And I have a big day tomorrow—a manicure!" She waggled her fingers at him. "I'd better go on up to bed."

I'll come with you. The words formed in his mind before he even realized it. Thank God he didn't say them.

"Good night." She gave him a bright smile, then vanished up the stairs.

Finn raked a hand through his hair. "Good grief, MacCauley," he muttered. "Get a life."

"Damn it, Tracy. Stop scratching." Finn jerked his head out from behind the camera and glowered at supermodel Tracy Holborn. "They aren't paying you a thousand dollars an hour to scratch your belly."

"They aren't paying me a thousand dollars an hour, period." Tracy pouted at him. "I can't help it if there are mosquitoes." It was one of the joys of shooting on location—putting up with all that nature had to offer.

"There are no mosquitoes in New York," Finn told her firmly, ducking behind the camera again.

"That's bull," Tracy retorted, wrinkling her nose and swatting again.

"Mind over matter, sweetheart." Finn said unsympathetically. "Give me a sultry look. Not quite so much pout." He scowled into the camera again, trying to find the mood. He was shooting a specialty catalogue of clothes for professional women. It was called *Urban Jungle*, but without megabucks, Central Park was as close to jungle as they were going to get. Still, it was his job to make it seem jungly—dangerous and hot and very, very green. It was Tracy's job to look like dynamite in the clothes. She was squirming again.

"Okay, okay. Stop and scratch." He waited until she was ready, then drew a deep breath. "Now give me more shoulder. Dip it down. Drop your chin a little. That's it. Perfect!"

"Her hair's mussed," the stylist protested, moving into camera range to fuss with it.

"Leave it!" Finn barked. "It's supposed to be mussed, damn it. This is a jungle. Her hair's fine. She's fine." He shot, moved, then shot again. And again. The stylist grumbled. Finn clicked the shutter, adjusted, clicked again. More.

"I don't want to!" He heard a childish protest somewhere behind him, breaking the mood.

He ignored it, continuing to shoot. "That's right. More lip. Let me see the tip of your tongue. That's it. Yeah." He ran his tongue over his own lips.

"Why can't we go with you?" the same childish voice demanded.

"Yeah. Why can't we? *He* doesn't want us. He yells at us."

"He doesn't yell at you," a soft feminine voice countered. "Not very often, anyway."

"He *hates* us. Please, Izzy. Pu-leeze?"

Izzy?

The childish voices took on sudden meaning.

What the hell was she doing here?

Finn spun around, disbelieving. Sure enough, there she was with Pansy and Tansy clutching either hand.

"Mrs. Strong is ill," Izzy said. "So I brought them to you."

"What?" He thought he'd misheard her.

"I went to the studio for the manicure as you commanded—" she made a face at him "—and I found out Mrs. Strong isn't there today. So if you want me to get this manicure, you'll have to watch the girls."

"I'm in the middle of a shoot."

"So I see. Fine. Then I won't go. It's okay with me. You can call your friend and tell her so."

And Carlota would have his head on a plate. She was making a special trip into the city today to do Izzy's hands. She had fussed and fumed, then agreed when

Finn reminded her of favors owed. She wouldn't like coming in again. *She wouldn't come in again!* And as temperamental she was, she wouldn't be thrilled about having to deal with two little girls while she was doing Izzy's hands.

Finn scowled, trapped. One look at his nieces and he could tell they felt the same way. He glared at them. One took a step back. The other—Tansy, no doubt—stuck her tongue out at him. He felt like sticking his out in return. He sighed. "All right. Leave them."

Izzy tried to free her hands from the girls' grasp. They clung like limpets. "Go on now. He's waiting," she said.

"Is not!" said the tongue sticker stoutly.

"I wanna go with you!" wailed the other one, clinging fast.

"What the hell's going on?" the catalog rep demanded, bustling up, poking a pencil in Finn's face. "We aren't shooting little girls, are we?"

The twins' eyes widened worriedly.

"Not yet," Finn said grimly.

Izzy gave him a steely disapproving look.

"Ooh, aren't they darling?" the hairstylist cooed. "Look at that hair. Did you ever see such a color. And the curl! I could do such wonderful things with that curl."

"Sierra cut it for us," Tansy said.

"I can do a better job than Sierra," the stylist sniffed.

"Great." Finn would take professional rivalry if he couldn't find a baby-sitter. "You do that. And watch them at the same time."

The stylist looked astonished. "Watch them? But who are they?"

"My nieces." He looked at Izzy and jerked his head in the stylist's direction. " Give 'em to her."

Izzy looked doubtfully at the frizzy-haired woman in skintight fuchsia spandex shorts and lime green smock. But Midge, the stylist, apparently accepted the challenge for she met Izzy halfway. The girls, shooting Finn wary glances all the while, put their hands in hers.

"Do you ever get purple fingers?" he heard Tansy ask.

"Sierra gots purple fingers," Pansy confided.

Finn could see the wheels turning in Midge's head. Izzy, looking like a mother abandoning her charges to a kindergarten class run by Attila the Hun, shot him one last speaking glance, then wrung her hands, turned and bolted away.

The catalog rep protested. "We can't have this. These children can't be here."

Finn fixed her with a baleful look. "No?"

The rep took a step backward. "The distraction... surely you can't work with distractions?"

"What the hell do you think you are?" He was gratified when her cheeks turned red. She huffed nervously and snapped her pencil in two.

"Sit down and stop jumping around," Finn said to her. "The sooner you get out of the way, the faster we can get this wrapped up."

"But—"

"You're bothering me again," he said silkily. "They're not bothering me." He glanced at the twins who now clung to Midge's hands and watched in rapt fascination. "Are you?" he asked them pointedly.

Two heads shook in solemn denial.

"See?" he said to the ad exec. "If you'd follow their example..."

She got the point.

Everyone got the point. No one did anything to slow things down—least of all the twins. They sat as still as church mice on the rock where Midge had put them, watching every move he made in complete silence and total absorption.

Knowing they were there, staring at him, waiting in morbid anticipation for him to take a bite out of someone for breakfast, kept him totally focused on Tracy. Having Midge fuss with the girls' hair was a stroke of genius, though. It prevented her from rushing to rearrange Tracy's hair after every clothing change. And the catalog rep, who apparently shared the twins' notion that Finn might at any moment revert to cannibalism, was so cowed that she didn't move until Finn shot the last roll and said, "That's it."

He straightened and flexed his shoulders, and became suddenly aware that he'd been working flat out for over two hours. The twins, with upswept spiky hairdos, were right where he left them. He did a double take, gave them a curt nod of approval, then went to pack up.

He was almost finished—would have been, if he could only find the damn lens cap—when he sensed someone standing next to his elbow. He glanced around.

Solemn green eyes, elbow height, stared into his. A small hand was thrust out toward him. "You dropped this." It was the lens cap.

He took it from her, half expecting her to flinch away. She didn't. Undoubtedly it was Tansy. He fitted the cap over the lens. "Thank you."

She nodded gravely. "You're welcome." Even then she didn't move away, but stood watching every move he made.

When he'd shut the lid to the camera case, he looked over at her. "You're not scared anymore?"

"Never was," she said stoutly.

No, from what he'd seen of Tansy, she probably wasn't. She reminded him of himself as a child—obstinate, determined, with more courage than brains. He gave her a faint smile.

"Pansy is, though," she confided after a moment. "She doesn't like it when you yell. She's not really a fraidy-cat. Most of the time, anyway. Mama says she's...artistic."

Finn's tongue traced a circle inside his cheek. "Artistic?"

"She imagines things."

"I'll bet," Finn said dryly.

"She does. An' she draws 'em. And paints. She's a better painter than I am."

"You don't like to paint?"

Tansy shrugged. "I'm not good at it."

"What are you good at?"

"Swimming. And climbing."

"And framing ogres?" Finn said with a small smile. A hint of a smile flickered across her face, too, then disappeared as if she wasn't sure whether to trust him with it. "Yes," she said firmly. "An' Uncle Hewey says I can really throw a baseball."

Uncle Hewey? Was he the man in Meg's life before Roger? Or was he one of Izzy's sailors? He couldn't remember and didn't think Tansy was the right person to ask.

He'd never had a conversation like this with a child. He couldn't remember ever having a conversation of any kind with a child. Not since he was one—and he'd done his best to get over childhood as quickly as possible.

"Can you bat?" he asked her.

She nodded. "I'm not very good, though."

"You'd probably get better with practice."

"I'd rather swim."

"Maybe we can go swimming."

"We went swimming with Izzy and Grandad."

Finn frowned. "Grandad?"

"He was Izzy's really, but he let us call him that, too."

Finn remembered the grandfather of one of his foster brothers inviting him to call him Grandpa. He'd stubbornly refused. Why bother? he'd thought. In a matter of months he'd be gone.

Now he wondered if maybe he hadn't been a little too stubborn, for even when Tansy said sadly, "He died," she didn't sound angry, only sad.

"I know. That's too bad."

"He was the bestest grandad in the whole world. Izzy said so. He took care of her since she was little. She didn't have a dad, either. Or a mom."

At least she'd been left to the "bestest grandad in the whole world," instead of an incompetent unwilling uncle. A look at Tansy's face showed him that her thoughts seemed to be running along the same lines.

He felt a pang of remorse for his gruff treatment of her and her sister. God knew it wasn't their fault Meg was so useless as a mother, nor that she had the misfortune to have him as her only living, semiresponsible relative.

"I'm hungry," he said, straightening up. "Are you?"

"A little."

"Do you like pizza?"

"Pizza's good."

"Think Pansy'd like some, too? Shall we ask her?"

"She'd like some," Tansy said. "You don't have to ask her." She stepped between Finn and her sister as if she could protect her from him.

"I won't yell," Finn promised.

Tansy turned to her sister, who still hadn't moved from her perch on the rock. "He won't yell," she said, just as if Pansy hadn't heard the words herself.

Pansy gave a tiny, jerky nod of her head.

"All right," Tansy said to Finn.

He straightened up. "Come on, then." He shouldered his camera bags. "Maybe after we can go swimming."

Tansy was the only one of the three of them daring enough to take a risk. When she'd handed him the lens cap, she'd done that. And somehow seeing a six-year-old girl with more courage to face reality than he had, had made Finn stop and think about someone other than himself.

So when they survived eating pizza together, he said, "How about going to the beach?"

"The beach?" The girls looked at each other doubtfully.

"Did you bring bathing suits?" he asked.

"Dunno." Tansy shrugged. Pansy looked worried.

A quick trip back to the apartment and a rummaging through their duffels had proved they hadn't.

"I guess we can't go then," Tansy said, looking crest-fallen now that the chance seemed to be evaporating.

"I bet they sell bathing suits somewhere in the city." Tansy brightened at once. "Really?"

He held out his hand. "Come on."

Tansy took it. Pansy didn't. But at least she followed along.

A sporting goods store a few blocks away on Broadway had exactly what they were looking for. Finn, used to seeing the world's most gorgeous women parading in front of his camera lens in less-is-more bathing suits, found himself smiling as the girls had picked their way through an entire rack full, debating hotly before deciding on the ones they wanted and trying them on to show him. Tansy was eager from the first, and even Pansy found one that she liked.

"Beautiful," he told them both. And he wasn't exaggerating. In fact he was half tempted to whip out his camera and take a few shots. The girls weren't old enough to be self-conscious yet, nor did they preen. Their blossoming joy was natural. He was enchanted.

Once they'd found what they liked, they were ready to go.

"How far is it?" Tansy skipped beside him. "Are we gonna walk?"

"We're taking the train," he told them, explaining that the subway was easier than driving would be. Tansy was eager. Pansy looked a little apprehensive still.

"We have one more stop to make," he said and led them into a small art supply store where he bought a sketch pad and a box of bold-colored markers, which he presented to Pansy.

She took them wordlessly, her eyes round and questioning.

He felt a moment's panic that he'd done the wrong thing. "Tansy says you're a good artist."

"She is," Tansy said stoutly.

A smile like he'd never seen before lit her sister's face. "Thank you," Pansy said softly, clutching the pad and markers against her chest. And she looked at him for the first time without that glimmer of wariness in her eyes.

Before the afternoon was over, Finn found out just how right Tansy was.

While she dashed and jumped and cavorted in the water, Pansy got her feet wet briefly, then retired to her towel where she stayed, drawing intently for the rest of the afternoon. She drew kids and dogs, swimmers and sunbathers, splashers and dashers. All simple, yet bold and exciting. In her own way she seemed able to catch the excitement that Tansy was so much a part of. The one did, the other observed.

Finn did both. He swam with Tansy. He shot pictures of them both. And for the first time since they'd walked through his studio door, he thought they might actually make a go of it after all.

On the way home they both fell asleep. Tansy, exhausted, sank into a deep slumber almost before they'd rattled out of the station. Pansy took a bit longer, starting to draw a picture of the people in their car, when she began to yawn. Minutes later she slumped against Finn's arm, her sketch pad slipping toward the floor.

He rescued it, then shifted so that he could sit with an arm around each of them. They were sticky and scratchy and sandy. Their spiky Midge-created hairdos had vanished in the water. All three of them probably looked like they'd been run over by a bus. Finn smiled. Izzy would be proud of him.

"We went on a subway!" Tansy said, bounding through the front door.

"To the beach!" Pansy added, her eyes as bright as Izzy had seen them since they'd arrived the week before. She'd been worried out of her mind when she'd come back from her manicure and Finn and the girls were nowhere to be seen. She'd called the studio and got the answering machine. She'd gone out and looked around the neighborhood. Then she'd come back and paced for the next four hours. And they'd been to the beach!

"Swimming!" Tansy said.

"An' I made you a picture!" Pansy looked over her shoulder at Finn who was just coming in behind the two bedraggled girls, looking pretty shattered himself, like a pirate who'd been keelhauled. "He's got it," she told Izzy.

Izzy steadied herself from the girls' onslaught and looked at Finn once more. No, not entirely shattered. There was something of a satisfied glow about him. Even as she thought it, he gave her a slow devastatingly attractive smile as he reached into his shirt pocket and took out a paper to hand to her. "Voilà," he said with a faint bow.

Izzy, fumbling, took the picture from his hand.

It was clearly recognizable as a Pansy MacCauley original. In her own vivid style the little girl had used bold colored markers to draw a beach crowded with swimmers and sunbathers and multicolored umbrellas. The detail was wonderful—the little boy with the sand pail; the children building a castle at the water's edge; the small black dog that seemed to be yapping at the heels of a pair of lovers walking arm in arm.

"Why, Pansy," Izzy exclaimed. "I can see it just as if I'd been there."

Tansy went up on tiptoe and poked at one vivid figure. "That one's me," she said, pointing out a carrot-topped child way out in the water.

"You swam way out there?" Izzy's eyes widened.

"Not alone," Tansy assured her, clearly aware from Izzy's tone that she was worried. She poked at the black-haired man next to the carrot-top. "That's Uncle Finn."

Uncle Finn. She hadn't heard the girls call him that yet. He'd just been *he,* up till now. Or *the ogre.* Izzy looked at him again speculatively.

"She said she liked to swim." Finn's blue eyes met hers for an instant, then slid away, almost as if Tansy's apparent affection embarrassed him. "Come on," he said gruffly to the girls. "You need baths, both of you. You smell like wet dogs."

Pansy's mouth formed an astonished O. Tansy just giggled and, grabbing her sister's hand, tugged her toward the stairs.

Izzy watched them go, then turned to stare at Finn.

"What're you looking at?" he growled, then stalked toward the kitchen.

"Dr. Jekyll and Mr. Hyde, I think." She smiled.

"You told me to try to get along. I did what you said." He shrugged irritably, then bent to rummage in the refrigerator. "Tansy said she liked swimming," he added gruffly. "And she said Pansy liked to draw."

Izzy, watching him, realized just how much of his grouchy exterior was no more than skin-deep.

Finn turned back and popped the top on a bottle of beer. He scowled at her. "What?" he demanded. He held out another bottle to her questioningly.

She shook her head. "No, thanks." Her smile broadened. "You're a very kind man."

"I'd offer anyone a beer."

"That's not what I meant, and you know it. I meant that you were kind to the girls."

He snorted and took a long draft from the bottle, then wiped his mouth on the back of his hand. "It was the least I could do."

"The least you could do was bring them back here and ignore them for the rest of the day. Or stick them with a baby-sitter," Izzy pointed out.

"I got the feeling they've been with enough baby-sitters. Besides, I'm not a complete ogre, despite what Pansy thinks."

"I'm sure she doesn't think so anymore," Izzy said gently. "Where did you take them? I never associate beaches with New York City."

"Ever heard of Coney Island?" He gave a grim smile. "It was a zoo, half the damn city was there. But—" he shrugged "—they seemed to like it."

"I imagine they had a ball."

"Yeah, well, like you said, it was better than bringing them back here. What the hell would I do with them here? I don't know what to do with kids."

"Seems to me you do."

Finn shook his head. "Nope." He finished that beer and snagged another. "Sure you don't want one?"

"No, thank you."

"You don't drink? Why not? Doesn't Sam approve?" There was a slightly belligerent tone to his voice that surprised her.

She cocked her head. "Are you by chance trying to pick a fight with me?" She thought his cheeks flushed slightly, but his face was sunburned enough so she couldn't tell.

"Maybe." He flicked her a quick glance. "Is it working?"

Izzy grinned. "No."

Finn rubbed a hand through his hair, then down his face. "Can't win for losing, can I?"

Something in his gaze when he looked at her again made her heart kick over. She tried to ignore it. "Are you trying to increase your ogre quotient, Mr. MacCauley?"

Finn's eyes met hers and awareness seemed suddenly to crackle between them. He shook his head. "Frankly, Miss Rule, I don't know what the hell I'm doing."

CHAPTER FIVE

THAT night she had the strangest dream. She was playing in the surf at Stinson Beach, racing after Sam who had been teasing her, splashing her, then dashing away and daring her to catch him. And so she ran, and he dodged and slipped. And she caught him—tackled him, as a matter of fact—brought him down on the sand so that their bodies pressed together from knee to neck.

"Got you!" she'd cried.

And he'd rolled over with her in his arms—and it wasn't Sam at all.

It was Finn.

Izzy jerked awake, trembling, and sat up, dragging in deep lungfuls of air, trying desperately to slow the rampaging of her heart.

Sam! Where are you, Sam? The words pounded in her head. She wrapped her arms around her drawn-up knees, hugging them tightly, wishing for a glimpse of his crooked grin or a touch from his hand, anything to banish the memory of Finn MacCauley still so vivid in her mind. Even if she wasn't ready to plunge into Sam's wealthy world, it seemed suddenly the safer alternative.

Why on earth had she dreamed of Finn?

There came the sudden sound of a door creaking and Izzy glanced up nervously to see her halfway closed door opening.

A small figure in a pale nightgown appeared. "Are you a'right, Izzy? Did you have a bad dream?"

Izzy took one last shuddering breath, then shook her head. "No, Pansy. I'm fine. Truly."

"I heard you say somethin'."

"I must have been talking in my sleep. I'm okay. Really. But it was good of you to come and ask."

"You come when I have bad dreams," Pansy said. She'd had two in the first days after their arrival in New York. Scary dreams, she'd told Izzy, where ogres yelled at her. Izzy hadn't had any trouble imagining what the ogre had looked like. Each time she had cuddled the little girl in her arms until Pansy had drifted off to sleep once more.

Now Pansy moved toward the bed and stood looking at Izzy worriedly in the moonlight. "I was thinking," she began slowly. She chewed on her thumbnail.

"What about?"

The little girl hesitated, then blurted, "What if I have a bad dream and you're not here?"

I will be here, Izzy wanted to say, but she couldn't. She knew it wasn't true. When Sam got back, she'd be gone.

And the sooner that happened, the better, she thought now. Especially if she was going to be dreaming about Finn.

"Your uncle will be here."

Pansy didn't reply. That was, in fact, something of an improvement. Before he'd taken them to the beach, Izzy was sure Pansy would have said, "Don't want him," in no uncertain terms.

"Mommy's not coming back, is she?"

Oh, damn, Izzy thought. Why now? Why me? Why hadn't Meg told them herself? Or why hadn't Finn?

But fairness wouldn't allow her to blame Finn. He'd been as much a victim of Meg's decisions as the girls were.

"No, dear. She isn't."

"Why? Doesn't she want us?"

"I think she would love to have you with her," Izzy said honestly. "But she knows she can't provide a good place for you. And she thinks your uncle can."

Pansy climbed onto the bed and Izzy slipped an arm around her narrow shoulders. She felt the unevenness of Pansy's breathing. "Thought so," Pansy said finally in a small voice. "He's okay," she added after a moment.

Izzy breathed a sigh of relief. "Yes," she said. "He is."

She wouldn't have said that a week ago. But she was beginning to get a pretty good idea that Finn MacCauley, for all his gruffness, wasn't the ogre Tansy had thought he was. She also knew, whether he really wanted to or not, that he wouldn't turn his back on them.

"Be better if you were here," Pansy said, giving Izzy a jolt. "Can't you stay?"

"You know the answer to that. Don't forget about Sam." And she found that she was saying it as much for her own benefit as for Pansy.

"I know. I like Sam, too." Pansy slanted Izzy a glance. "Maybe you an' Sam could adopt us."

"I would love having you for my children," Izzy told the little girl. "But I don't think that's what your mother had in mind."

"She wouldn't care."

"Your uncle would."

Pansy tilted her head so that her eyes looked deeply into Izzy's. "Truly?"

"Yes," Izzy said softly, but firmly. "Give him a chance to prove it to you."

A minute went by, then another. Finally Pansy gave a small, almost imperceptible nod of her head.

"Sam's coming home the day after tomorrow," she told Finn the next evening when he got home from work.

Still haunted by her dream, she'd called his office first thing in the morning and learned the good news.

"Tomorrow?" Finn's black brows drew down. He kicked off his shoes and socks and padded barefoot to the kitchen.

Izzy followed him. "Don't worry. I won't leave you totally in the lurch. I'll take the girls with me for the time being." She'd decided this afternoon that Sam wouldn't mind, and it was the perfect solution.

Finn started to open the refrigerator. He turned instead and looked at her over his shoulder. "Take them with you? What's that mean?"

"During the days. Sam won't care and—"

"I thought you were terrified to set foot in Fletcher's apartment. I thought you were quaking in fear of his mother. And now you're going to drag two little kids with you? Did you have a conversion experience?"

Izzy started to bite her thumbnail, then remembered all the trouble Carlota had expended to shape them up. She jammed her hands into the pockets of her baggy shorts. "I found courage."

Or something else that scared her more. Even now— if she dared—Izzy could remember the hard muscled feel of Finn's body beneath hers in her dream.

He snorted. "Yeah. Probably hidden in the depths of those damn shorts." He popped the top on a can of beer and took a long swallow. But even with his head tipped back, Izzy could still see his disparaging look.

She stiffened. "I told you, I'll get other clothes!"

He wiped his mouth on the back of his hand. "Yeah, you will. Tomorrow. You can bring the girls down to the studio first thing in the morning and Anita will take you shopping."

"I don't—"

"We have a deal, Miz Rule. Tomorrow. Nine-thirty sharp."

No one was going to say Finn MacCauley didn't keep his part of a bargain. So if Isobel Rule could hardly wait to leave, fine, she could leave. But she was going to leave looking like she could knock 'em on their Upper East Side asses.

He called on Anita, a clothing stylist whom he trusted wouldn't bring Izzy home with Day-Glo miniskirts and see-through blouses—although a part of him wondered just exactly what Sam Fletcher would say if she did—and arranged for her to take Izzy shopping.

"She'll know what you need," he told Izzy. "She needs everything," he told Anita.

"I can't afford everything," Izzy told her. The look she gave him told Finn that offering to pay for it himself wouldn't set well at all.

"Anita won't spend a dollar herself where a dime will do."

"Count on it," Anita said with a bright smile. "Come on, kiddo. We've got work to do."

"How come we can't go?" the girls wanted to know.

"Because you need to help me here," Strong told them.

"And me," Finn said.

Their heads whipped around and they looked at him, eyes wide. Izzy stopped halfway out the door.

Finn gave her a defiant look, then turned his gaze back on the girls. "Come with me," he said to the twins and was gratified to hear Izzy go out.

Pansy had done paper dolls with old prints Strong had given her the last time she was here. They were leftovers from the previous day's shooting. But if she wanted a little variety, well, he had a back room full of prints that

never passed muster. He led the little girl in and waved
a hand. "It's all yours," he told her and he handed her
a pair of scissors.

Pansy positively gaped.

"You can give us a fashion show after," he said.

"Really?" She flashed him that grin again, the one
that had almost knocked him over the first time he saw
it.

"You don't want to cut out fashions," he said to
Tansy. "You come with me."

She gave him a wary look, but then shrugged and followed. He led her into the reception room and picked
up the camera she'd been fiddling with on the first day.
Then, taking her back into the studio, he pointed her
toward a tall stool near his camera. "Sit up there."

She sat. He got out a roll of film and opened the
camera. Carefully, slowly, while Tansy watched his every
move, he proceeded to load it. He didn't close the back.
Then he took the film out again and held it out to her.
"Now you do it."

She stared. But when he didn't move, just kept holding
out the film and camera, she tried to do what he had
done. She got pretty far before she needed him to show
her the next step. When he showed her, she did it. Then
he said, "Close it up." She did.

"My first shoot's going to be here in about ten
minutes," he told her. "If you stay out of the way, you
can shoot, too."

Tansy's mouth dropped open.

Finn winked at her. "Gotta start somewhere," he said.

Finn was right about one thing—Anita knew her stuff
and she wouldn't spend a dime, let alone a dollar, when
a penny would do. She also took Finn's com-
mission seriously.

"He says you need to knock their socks off," she told Izzy. "Well, actually—" she giggled "—he was a little more graphic than that."

Izzy didn't think she needed to knock anyone's socks off, unless it might be Sam's, but there was no dissuading Anita. So she just followed along as Anita dragged her from showroom to showroom along Seventh Avenue, trying on whatever Anita told her to, sucking her stomach in, pushing her boobs out.

"One little basic black dress," Anita decreed, studying Izzy's curves and short stature. "A knit, maybe a little skimpy, you know, to show off those curves."

Izzy hadn't ever paid much attention to her curves.

"Nothing boxy. No cinches at the waist. And definitely no checks and plaids," Anita went on, wrinkling her nose at the plaid bermudas Izzy was wearing. "Ever."

Izzy swallowed. "Right."

Anita picked colors, too. Golds and russets and deep cerulean blues that both complemented Izzy's skin tones and brought out her eyes. "There. See," she said when she had Izzy decked out in a pair of jeans and blazer that did all those things *and* made her seem taller. "Isn't that great?"

Izzy had to admit it was. Jeans were jeans as far as she was concerned. And a blazer—well, she'd never had one, but.... "I can't spend an arm and a leg."

"You buy a few basics," Anita said briskly. "Then we work from there."

They finished on Seventh Avenue, then headed down to another place Anita knew near the World Trade Center. "Great prices," she confided. "You'll love it."

Izzy's head spun, but she allowed herself to be towed. There they bought more jeans and black turtlenecks, a pair of Gucci loafers and Doc Martens combat boots.

"Combat boots?"

"Absolutely. Great with jeans. Hurry up. We need to run over to Soho to a jeweler I know. You need earrings. Chunky silver ones. They'll be wonderful with that hair."

By the time Anita had finished with her, they had so many bags and boxes Izzy felt like a character in a regency novel just outfitted for the season—either that or a pack animal on a Himalayan trek.

Anita helped her carry all of it back to the elevator going to the studio, but declined to come up. "Can't. Got a hot date." She flashed Izzy a grin. "Besides, you don't need me now. I did my bit. Go on up and knock 'im dead."

Izzy barely managed to lift a finger to push the button. Her feet hurt. Her mind spun. She told herself it was exhaustion. She told herself she needed a moment to catch her breath.

The fact was she felt nervous. Anita had told her half a dozen times in the last four hours that she was lovely, beautiful, stunning. And in the enthusiasm of the moment, Izzy had allowed herself to believe.

Now she didn't.

And Finn MacCauley wouldn't, either.

She didn't know why she cared. She didn't know why it mattered.

She might be dreaming about him, but he couldn't have cared less about her. He was only doing this because of the deal they'd made. What she looked like made no difference to him at all.

So why had she spent all afternoon picking out clothes that she thought Finn MacCauley would like?

Deep down she knew she had done exactly that. She'd listened to Anita, considered Anita's advice, studied Anita's suggestions. But whenever she'd had to make a choice, she'd always asked herself, what would Finn like?

What did she care what Finn MacCauley liked?

What mattered was what *Sam* liked...what would make her feel comfortable when she ventured into his world.

Just remember that, she admonished herself. *Remember that.* She repeated it—like a mantra—as the elevator door slid open and she pushed the buzzer outside Finn's studio door.

Strong and the girls were there, Pansy surrounded by a cutout wardrobe that put Izzy's new togs to shame, and Tansy with the lineup of the San Francisco Giants in a row. They looked up expectantly.

"You're not wearing anything new," Tansy said accusingly.

"No," Izzy said, dragging in the first load. "I'm carrying it. Come out and help me bring it in."

"Not necessary," said a male voice, and she looked around to see Finn emerge from the door to his studio. "We'll just take it on home." He didn't even bat an eye at all her packages. "Give me those," he said, and swept them out of her arms. She looked up at him, startled and extremely aware of his sudden closeness. But then just as quickly, he moved away again, getting the girls to clean up their projects, then herding them toward the door.

"It was a success, I take it," Finn said, bundling Izzy, the girls and all the parcels into a cab.

"What do you think?" Izzy said dryly.

Finn grinned and her stomach did a flip. "I knew I could count on Anita."

Izzy settled back into the far corner of the cab. "She's amazing. She knows everywhere to buy everything in New York."

"She's made shopping an art form." He looked at her curiously as the cab pulled out into traffic. "You look dead."

"Thank you very much." She shot him a malevolent glance.

"I'm just surprised," he admitted. "I thought you'd love it. Most women would."

"Are you implying that I'm not normal?"

The grin slashed across his face again. "Well, maybe just a little."

Izzy sighed. "You're right. I'm not. It was...fun. But it wore me out."

"Not too worn out to model for us this evening?"

She stared at him. He gave her a hopeful look.

"Please!" Tansy begged.

And Pansy said, "You'll be like one of my paper dolls."

Izzy felt her cheeks warm. "I can't. I need to cook supper."

"I'll cook," Finn said.

"He'll cook," Tansy said.

Pansy nodded her head. "We'll help." All three of them smiled at her. She was stuck.

When they got to Finn's brownstone, he chivvied her up toward the bathroom to take a shower. "I'll have supper ready when you're finished. Just throw on a robe. We'll have the fashion show after."

Throw on a robe? Izzy stared at him, askance. She knew it was only in her mind that being so close to naked around Finn would be an issue. He saw far more beautiful women than she in various stages of undress all the time. But still...

"Come on, Izzy!" the girls prompted, dragging her toward the stairs. Helpless, Izzy went with them.

*   *   *

Anita had, indeed, not let him down.

As Izzy came slowly down the stairs in a curve-hugging knit black dress that was so simple it was stunning, Finn sucked in his breath. Used to the leggy exotic look of the models who tripped in and out of his studio all day long, Izzy's more compact, almost elfin beauty made him stand up straight. It also made him adjust the fit of his jeans.

She stopped before she got all the way down. "There," she said, almost defiantly. "You've seen it." She started back up again.

"Come here."

She looked at him, her eyes wide and wary. "What? Why?"

"Because I haven't seen it all."

"There's not much to see. There's hardly any dress. You'd think they'd give you more material if they're going to charge these exorbitant prices." She started up the steps again.

"Izzy! Come down here."

She turned again, glaring at him. Then slowly, reluctantly she came the rest of the way down the steps, stopped and stared at him.

He slid one hand into his pocket. "Turn around."

She did a quick pirouette, then headed toward the stairs again.

He reached out and caught her hand, pulling her back. Her fingers were warm and damp in his, and he hung on longer than he had any right to.

He didn't care. He'd waited all day to get a glimpse of Isobel Rule in something other than a baggy faded T-shirt and a pair of two sizes too big Bermuda shorts. He was going to look his fill.

He kept a hold on her, allowing her only their arms' length while he looked her over. He started at her toes and worked his way up. It was a scenic trip. His gaze lingered here and there—at the hem just above her knees, at the flare of her hips, at the indentation of her waist and the thrust of her breasts. It spent a fair amount of time at the neckline, and he found himself wishing that it plunged just a little more. His eyes met hers. Her face was flushed.

"You're embarrassed?"

"Yes." The word came as a hiss from between her teeth. She was still trying to pull her hand out of his grasp.

He smiled and raised her fingers to his lips. He meant the gesture to be teasing, mocking perhaps, though whether her or himself he couldn't have said. But, regardless of what he'd intended, the brush of his lips against the soft warmth of her skin sent a jolt right through him. It seemed to have a definite effect on Izzy, too, for she snatched her hand away, rubbing it against the fabric of the dress.

Goaded, Finn couldn't help taunting. "Doesn't Sam kiss you like that?"

Still trying to pull away, she shook her head, not answering.

"How does he kiss you?"

Izzy ran her tongue over her lips and looked away. "None of your business."

"How about like this?" He should have been calling himself a fool even as he did it, but he didn't stop to think. He simply pulled her into his arms, touched his lips to hers, and began to kiss her with all his considerable expertise, desire, and every bit of the longing that had been building for what seemed like years.

God knew he'd been a long time without a woman in his life. He hadn't had the time—or the inclination—recently to look beyond the lens of his camera. An appreciation of Angelina Fiorelli's lips was as close as he'd come. All his energy had been absorbed by his work.

But now his work wasn't enough. Maybe this niggling desire had begun with his fascination with Angelina's lips. Maybe it had started before. Or maybe it hadn't really blossomed until Isobel Rule with her peachy skin and her outrageous baggy shorts and T-shirts had turned up in his life. But whatever and however it had begun, there was no question about who it focused on now.

And why not Izzy? She was there every day, prancing around his apartment, giggling with the girls, telling them stories, fixing meals, sprawling on the floor playing games, running her fingers through her pert new hair cut. Driving him to distraction.

And damn it, yes, he was distracted. All day long he'd been distracted. All week long—ever since she'd come—he'd been distracted.

So he was exorcising her. Getting her out of his system. But kissing Izzy didn't seem to be exorcising her at all. On the contrary, the taste of her seemed like a vortex drawing him in. He'd expected she would stiffen, tense, then pull away from him. She didn't. Her body softened, molding itself to his. Her lips parted, giving him access to the sweetness of her mouth. And Finn took advantage of her willingness. His arms went around her, drawing her body tight against him. His tongue slipped between her lips to stroke against hers. And when she responded eagerly he felt a shudder run through him.

"Ooh, look!"

"They're kissing!"

The childish voices jerked both of them back to earth with a thud. Izzy yanked herself out of his embrace and stared up at him with horrified eyes. Finn took a heaving breath, then another, and another.

The twins stared down from halfway up the steps in openmouthed astonishment. Then one of them said, ''I thought you were marryin' Sam.''

CHAPTER SIX

IT WAS the dress that had made him kiss her. Of course it was the dress! It certainly couldn't have been any attraction he felt for her personally; Izzy knew that well enough.

She smothered the almost hysterical laugh that threatened to bubble up inside her as she thought perhaps Anita could use Finn's actions as evidence of her ability as a stylist! If his reaction was anything to go by, Anita definitely knew her stuff.

Now, Izzy told herself, she hoped it had the same effect on Sam.

Tomorrow. Tomorrow she would see Sam.

Only twenty-four more hours and her world would be right side up again and all the pieces would be in their appropriate places. If Finn really didn't want her to take the girls with her temporarily, she might come and keep an eye on them until he found a permanent nanny. But she wouldn't have to stay here, wouldn't have to be in danger of turning around and finding him behind her, of looking up and connecting with his deep blue gaze. If she worked it right, she wouldn't even have to see him.

God knew she didn't want to see him.

She sat on her bed in the dark and pressed her hands to her cheeks, feeling them burn. They had been burning for the last two hours—ever since she'd felt his gaze on her as she came down the stairs in Anita's "basic black dress." Basic, Izzy thought, being the operative word. As in basic instincts. Finn's. And her own.

She didn't know what—if anything—he'd told the girls about their kiss. She hadn't been able to come up with much of an explanation.

In the face of their shocked expressions, she'd said, "I *am* marrying Sam. Your uncle and I, um, we, er...the dress..." But her voice was so shaky it didn't even sound like her own.

The girls didn't reply. They'd only continued to stare in amazement. Finally, Pansy had run her tongue over her lips as if trying to imagine how a dress could have inspired a kiss like that.

Izzy's own tongue traced her lips now. They trembled still with the memory of the way his lips had kissed them, tasted them—as she had tasted him.

If she could, perhaps, blame Finn's behavior on his seeing her in the dress, her own behavior wasn't quite so comprehensible.

She told herself she'd done it because she was missing Sam. She hadn't seen him since her grandfather's funeral three months before. And then he'd only been in the city overnight. Plus they'd hardly been in the mood for passion under the circumstances.

He'd held her, comforted her, doing his best to bolster her spirits and make her look toward the future. And he'd kissed her that night and again before he left on the plane the next morning.

But never in a million years had he kissed her the way Finn had.

Of course he hadn't! she reminded herself. Because Sam was gentle, discreet, thoughtful. In the five years she had known him, he'd never kissed her like that— not even when they'd got engaged. He certainly wouldn't have done so the night of her grandfather's funeral or the day after.

She wouldn't have expected him to.

But tomorrow... Tomorrow he would.

Izzy shut her eyes, trying to blot out the memory of Finn's lips, of his kiss, and prayed that tomorrow would hurry up and come.

"So, what'd you think of the dress?" Anita asked him the next morning as she handed one of the models the shirt the girl was supposed to put on, then slanted Finn a sly smiling glance as she pointed the girl toward the dressing room. "Pretty snazzy, huh?"

Finn grunted. He fiddled with his camera. He didn't need to fiddle with the camera. There was no earthly reason for him to fiddle with the camera—other than avoiding Anita's gaze.

She smiled. "She's a peach, your Izzy. She—"

"She's not *my* Izzy!" Finn snapped.

Anita's brows lifted. She gave him a long, speculative look. "Uh-huh," she said at last. "Got you."

He scowled. "What?"

Anita gave him a knowing smile. "She's got you. You're interested in her."

"She needs help. And so do I. I made a bargain with her."

"This has nothing to do with your so-called bargain," Anita said. The model reappeared, buttoning the shirt. Anita stood up and began to adjust it, making the girl look sexier. "And you know it," she said to Finn over her shoulder.

"I don't know what you're talking about," he said stiffly. He wished she would stop messing with the shirt and let him take pictures.

"Pull the other one while you're at it." Anita shook her head. "She's a pretty girl, Finn, and you know it. But she's more than a pretty girl. She's a nice girl."

He snorted. "What do you know about nice?"

"You'd be surprised," Anita said mildly. "I didn't always live in the fast lane. There's a lot of Oklahoma left in me. Enough to appreciate freshness when I see it. And your—sorry." She grinned. "Izzy is fresh and bright and fun. I can see why you're attracted."

"I'm not attracted. And she's engaged," Finn said dampeningly.

"She's not married, though. Not yet."

Finn scowled. "Engaged is close enough. To Sam Fletcher, for God's sake!" Anita—and everyone else in New York with any business savvy at all—knew Sam Fletcher.

"Really? Sam Fletcher, hm?" Anita considered that, then gave him a sympathetic smile. "Guess you've got your work cut out for you then."

It wasn't like that. It wasn't like that at all. He didn't want to take Izzy away from Sam Fletcher. Hell, what would he do with her once he got her?

A certain sudden tension in the seat of his masculinity answered that question promptly enough. Finn scowled as he stamped up the steps to his apartment. *Besides that,* he thought savagely. Hell, she couldn't leave soon enough to suit him!

He could hear the girls giggling upstairs when he came in. Izzy was talking on the phone. She sat on the kitchen table with her feet on one of the chairs. She was still wearing the ubiquitous chartreuse T-shirt, but the shorts at least were new. A deep peach color that complemented the honey tan of her legs. She waggled her fingers at him and grinned, then mouthed, "Sam!" and the grin widened.

Finn, expecting to feel an immediate lightening of spirit, was surprised to find he was only annoyed.

"No," Izzy was saying now. "I understand completely. No, not tonight. It's fine, Sam. Really. Jet lag is nothing to take lightly. Sleep tonight and by tomorrow you'll be raring to go."

Finn's jaw tightened. He kicked off his shoes and unbuttoned his shirt. It was sweltering in here, even with the windows open. He wondered why she didn't ever use the air-conditioning. He stripped his shirt off.

Izzy averted her eyes. "How early?" she said into the telephone. "Oh, I think that'd be fine. I'll see you in the morning, then." She made a kissing sound with her mouth, then, as if she suddenly remembered when she'd last been kissed, she stopped abruptly and stared at Finn, stricken.

Their gazes met; hers slid quickly away.

"I love you, Sam," she said, then she hung up and turned to face Finn. "Sam's got back this afternoon from Paris. He's exhausted so—"

"Poor guy," Finn said unsympathetically.

"So," Izzy went on firmly, "he won't be coming by until tomorrow. But he'll be picking me up at nine. I hope that's not too early."

"And what am I supposed to do with the girls?" he demanded.

"Nothing," Izzy said breezily. "We'll take them with us."

"What? Take them with you?"

She shrugged. "Well, I know you don't have to work tomorrow, but I didn't know if you'd made other plans, and I did agree to watch them until you got a nanny. Have you, by the way, set up any more interviews?"

"No."

She arched a brow. "Have you looked?"

"Of course." Not much, but she didn't have to know that. He would look. And soon. "How come you're willing to take them? I figured you'd be dying to fall into bed with Mr. Millionaire.''

"Just because you—'' She broke off, her words sputtering to a stop. Then, "Do you have to undress the instant you get in the house?'' she demanded, her eyes flicking from his face to his bare chest and back again.

A grin twisted Finn's mouth. "Why? Worried I'll turn you on? Again,'' he added nastily.

Izzy clutched her arms across her chest. "About last night...I never intended...that kiss wasn't—''

"No. It wasn't,'' he said, relenting in the face of her obvious dismay. "You didn't mean anything by it? Well, fine. I didn't mean anything by it either.''

"It was an aberration,'' Izzy said after a moment. She ran her tongue over her lips. "Right?''

"Right.''

"Good.'' She hugged herself and rocked back and forth on her heels, then gave a little giggle.

Finn shot her a hard look. "What's funny?''

"I was just thinking that maybe it was...the Finn MacCauley seal of approval?'' There was a tiny grin on her face as she said the words. But then it faded, and the look she gave him was equal parts innocence and hopefulness.

He felt that earlier very masculine tension snake through him and he turned away abruptly. "Maybe it was,'' he said gruffly. He glanced around, then focused on the childish noises coming from upstairs. "What are the girls up to?'' he asked. Then, "Never mind. I'll go see.''

It was a hell of a thing, he told himself, when things had deteriorated so badly that to avoid Izzy he found himself actually seeking the company of a pair of little girls.

*   *   *

She counted the minutes until Sam was due to arrive, keeping out of Finn's way for the rest of the evening, reading the girls stories and playing Go Fish until it was their bedtime, then retiring to her own room to read.

Or try to. But though she kept her eyes on her book, her mind seemed to be on the sound of Finn moving around downstairs. She didn't know what he was doing, but it seemed to involve a lot of pacing about, a little thumping of this and that, and the French doors being opened and closed. He left shortly after ten, right before she was going to shut off her light.

A late date? she wondered.

With which one of the bevy of beauties who surrounded him all day long? As far as she knew he hadn't had a date since she and the girls had been there. She didn't imagine for a minute that he was usually so solitary. She only had to look at the photos stored in the back of her closet to know he had a definite interest in the opposite sex.

She only had to remember the way he kissed her—

Drat! She didn't *want* to remember the way he kissed her.

She wanted Sam. In only a few more hours she would be seeing him again, touching him again. *Kissing* him again. She rolled over and hugged her pillow against her chest. She shut her eyes. She was afraid to go to sleep.

What if she dreamed about Finn?

She didn't remember what she dreamed—which she took as a good sign. She did know she had got blessed little sleep by the time the alarm went off at six and she got up to take a steamy bath. After, wrapping a bath sheet around her, she washed and dried her hair. She debated using the laminates that Sierra had told her would make her hair "move." She decided she'd rather have it in one place. She fluffed her fingers through it, and hoped Sam would like it as much as she did. Her hair was the best part of this whole makeover Finn had put her through.

The makeup was a different story. She put it on the way Tonio, a makeup artist friend of Finn's, had showed her the same day Carlota had given her the manicure. She used just the lightest foundation and only the tiniest bit of blush. Then she stared at herself in the mirror, trying to find the old Izzy Rule.

She tried to waggle her eyebrows, but they didn't waggle anymore. They arched now—"the way they're supposed to," Tonio had told her. "No one wants ugly thick caterpillars crawling across their face," he said flatly. "Do they?"

Izzy had never thought about her eyebrows like that before.

She picked up the lip liner he had chosen for her. It intimidated her. But she figured if she tried using it now, at least it was early enough that her hand wasn't shaking from nervousness. Yet.

She laid out first one outfit, then another, tempted by the basic black dress that had inspired Finn's kiss. Would it have the same effect on Sam?

Heaven help her, it better, Izzy thought. But nine on a Saturday morning of a day she was planning to spend with him and the girls didn't seem like the time to be trying out its charms.

So she opted for a pair of jeans, a French silk T-shirt in a shimmery russet color, and the chunky silver necklace and earrings that Anita had helped her pick out. But when she was all dressed, she still had an hour to go before Sam was to arrive.

She could hear Finn prowling around below, talking to the girls as they got out cereal and bowls and silverware. Ordinarily Izzy would be with them. Today she was lurking about in the upstairs hallway, feeling idiotic.

Go down, for goodness' sake, she told herself. What was she afraid of? He certainly wasn't going to kiss her again! Not when the infamous black dress was tucked safely away in the back of the closet.

What was it Grandad had always told her? "Gotta face your fears, Izzy, my girl. They just get bigger if you run away."

Izzy was quite sure she had no desire to face an even bigger-than-life Finn MacCauley. So she sucked in a deep breath and marched downstairs. She couldn't help remembering last night when she'd come down modeling the dress, and her knees quaked at the memory.

But just as she got low enough to see into the kitchen, Tansy made a wild gesture at the table and knocked over her milk. "Oh, no!"

"Oh, hell!" Finn glared at her.

"Here now," Izzy said soothingly, hurrying in, ignoring the way his gaze locked on her as she grabbed the roll of paper towels from the counter and bent to wipe up the milk. "It's all right, Tansy. Happens all the time. We'll get it mopped up in a second." She got on her knees with the paper towels, concentrating all her attention on the rapidly expanding puddle, and did her best to ignore the very masculine bare feet that managed to stay within the scope of her vision.

Suddenly a rag appeared in front of her face. She took it gratefully and flicked Finn a quick glance. "Thank you."

"Don't mention it." His tone was dry. He took the wadded-up sopping paper towels from her and threw them away.

Izzy mopped the area where the milk had spilled. Another damp rag appeared just when she needed it.

She took it. He held out his hand for the one she'd used.
She hesitated for a split second, then gave it to him and
kept mopping. A dry rag appeared. She used it, too. She
didn't know how long she'd have stayed down on the
floor if the downstairs doorbell hadn't rung.

Finn pushed the intercom button. "Who is it?"

There was a silence. Then, "Sam Fletcher."

Izzy scrambled to her feet. Finn shot her an unreadable look, then pushed the button to open the front
door. Izzy brushed at the knees of her jeans, ran her
fingers over her hair, licked her lips nervously.

"You look fine, damn it," Finn growled.

She could hear footsteps coming along the hallway
toward the door, then a knock. The girls ran to open it.

And there he was, tall and lean, and as dear and fam-
iliar and wonderful as ever. Izzy beamed at him.

He stood stock-still in the doorway and stared. *"I—
Izzy?"* His jaw seemed in danger of dragging on the
ground. "Is that—?"

"Don't tell me you don't recognize me."

He shut his mouth, swallowed, then raked a hand
through his sun-streaked brown hair and shook his head
slowly, looking dazed. "Took me by surprise," he admitted, a slow grin spreading across his cheerful face.
"What can I say? Wow." Then he opened his arms and
took a step forward.

Izzy flew into them, wrapping her arms around him,
hugging him fiercely, reveling in the comfortable strength
of his embrace, in the cool press of his cotton shirt
against her cheek and the brush of his freshly shaven
jaw on her temple. But it wasn't enough—this hug, this
desperate clinging.

She fused her mouth to his, seeking the jolt she'd
found last night in Finn's hungry kiss, in her own
sudden desire.

She saw Sam's eyes jerk open wide. He held the kiss for an instant, then wrapped his fingers around her upper arms and lifted her bodily away so that they stared into each other's eyes.

He sucked air, then gave a half laugh. "Not in front of the children," he said shakily.

Izzy flushed. "S-sorry." She lifted a hand to her cheek, self-conscious, not daring to look at Finn. "I . . . was just . . . it's been so long."

"Too long," Sam said, drawing her around so that he was able to slip his arm over her shoulders. "You really do look . . . wonderful." He sounded almost awestruck.

"Well, I didn't want you to be embarrassed by me so some of Finn's friends gave me some pointers." She wasn't about to tell him the details of their deal.

"Finn?" Sam said, his gaze flicking toward the man who was scowling at him from the kitchen. "Perhaps," he said to Izzy, "you ought to introduce us."

"Of course." Izzy felt her flush deepen. "Sam, this is the girls' uncle, Finn MacCauley. Finn—" she still didn't look at him "—this is Sam."

Sam held out a hand to Finn. "Pleased to meet you."

"Yeah." But there was certainly no reciprocal pleasure in Finn's tone. He dropped Sam's hand and folded his arms across his chest.

Sam kept on smiling. "Izzy says you're a photographer?"

Finn nodded curtly. The look on his face didn't encourage further discussion.

"For magazines?" Sam persisted.

Another nod.

"Fascinating. I bet you get to do a lot of traveling." He looked at Finn expectantly.

"No more than you."

Izzy could see Finn wasn't in one of his charming moods. She turned a bright smile on Sam and took hold of his hand. ''The girls and I are ready,'' she said. ''Shall we go?''

They started out the door. Then Tansy looked over her shoulder. ''Are you comin', Uncle Finn?''

''No.''

''No, he's not!'' Izzy said at the same time. Their eyes met for a split second, then Izzy jerked her glance away and herded the girls out the door.

Sam started to follow, then paused. ''Nice to have met you.''

Finn grunted. Over Sam's shoulder he gave Izzy one last steely look, then shut the door with a decided click in Sam's face.

Her fiancé turned and met Izzy's worried look. ''Not much of a morning person, is he?''

Sam took them to the Bronx Zoo—not precisely the sort of place a romantic reunion ought to take place, but with a pair of six-year-old twins in tow, romance wasn't exactly on the menu.

The four of them oohed and aahed over elephants and tigers, watched snow leopards both in slumber and on the prowl, peered across ravines separating them from hungry crocodiles and capped the afternoon off with a ride on a camel. They ate hot dogs and ice cream and giggled and laughed, and Sam gave each of the girls a ride on his shoulders when they were tired. He told Izzy all about his travels—the street bazaar in Bangkok, the silk merchant in Singapore, the pearl dealer in Hong Kong—in the same easy way he'd always told her about them when he'd passed through San Francisco.

And all the while she watched and listened, she thought, *I wish he'd kiss me again.* She tried to play

over in her mind the kiss they'd shared when he'd come
in the door that morning. She tried to remember the
caress of his lips, the crush of his mouth on hers, the
taste of him.

She kept remembering Finn.

The memory was like a double exposed film. You
could see one event, but not without seeing the other.
She told herself it was because she'd been so stunned,
so jarred by Finn's kiss that it had completely thrown
her. She hadn't been ready for Sam's—not completely
ready, so Finn's had intruded upon it.

But now—now she was. *Kiss me,* she thought. *Kiss
me again.*

But Sam was telling Pansy about some calligraphy on
rice paper that he had seen. And when he looked at Izzy,
he smiled and squeezed her hand, but he didn't look as
if kissing her was even on his mind.

She shouldn't expect it. Sam was a discreet sort of
guy—not one given to public displays of affection. He
was holding her hand in his. That was enough.

There would be time for more later. In private.
Without the girls. They were having dinner together, just
the two of them.

And then . . .

Izzy hugged to herself the thought of what was to
come. But she made herself focus on the moment, en-
joying it—just sitting on the bench and listening to Sam
talking, turning her face to the sun and feeling the tension
of the past couple of weeks begin, at last, to seep out
of her.

Sam was home. Now everything would be all right.

So she'd gone out to dinner with Fletcher? So what?

The guy wasn't an ax murderer.

He was one of the most successful, highly respected, wealthiest men in New York City. And a gentleman, to boot.

So why was he pacing the floor like a man who'd let his only daughter go out with the town rapist? Finn asked himself.

He didn't like any of the answers.

How the hell long did it take to have dinner anyway? He and the twins had had their dinner in less than an hour—and that counted walking all the way to the Korean grocery on Columbus and getting salad fixings and a pack of hot dogs, then coming back and fixing the meal themselves!

Of course it wasn't a five-course meal. But who said Sam Fletcher was taking Izzy out for a five-course meal? Who knew *what* they were doing?

But whatever it was, it didn't include him and the twins. They'd brought the girls back at six, tired and happy, and had told him they were on their way to dinner.

"You won't mind fixing them dinner, will you?" Izzy had said.

He'd grunted a reply with enough bad grace that she'd said, "You didn't have a date, did you? I guess we could stay here." She'd looked at Sam for confirmation.

But Finn had growled, "No, damn it, I don't have a date! Go on!" And if he'd banged around the kitchen all the time she was showering and getting ready, doing his best to ignore Sam Fletcher's well-meaning conversational attempts, well, too damn bad!

And he hadn't even acknowledged their departure because he had other things to do. It had been months since he'd defrosted the freezer! Could he help it if he was hacking furiously at a chunk of ice when they left?

But that had been just before seven. Hours ago. It was almost eleven now and they weren't back yet.

"Uncle Finn?"

He jerked up from the daybed where he'd finally slouched after pacing got him nowhere. There was a twin crouched on one of the steps of the spiral staircase, looking worriedly down at him. He frowned. "What's wrong?"

"Where's Izzy?"

He dragged in a deep breath. "She went out to eat, remember?"

"An' she's still gone?"

"It's not that late," Finn said quickly, exactly the opposite of what he'd just been thinking himself. But heaven knew the girls had had enough worry in their young lives just thanks to their mother—they didn't need more brought on by some thoughtless young woman who ought to know better.

"It's been hours."

"Listen, Tan—you are Tansy, aren't you?" he asked. She shook her head. "I'm P-Pansy."

That surprised him. He knew he'd been making a little progress with her. She'd begun smiling at him ever since their day at the beach. And she talked to him when her sister did. But she hadn't really engaged him in conversation by herself yet—until now.

Finn raked a hand through his hair as he stood and walked over toward the steps. "Well, listen, Pansy, your friend Izzy is a big girl. She can take care of herself. Besides, we didn't give her a curfew."

"What's a curfew?"

"A deadline. A time when she has to be home."

Pansy stuck her finger in her mouth, contemplating that notion. Then she pulled it out again and said forlornly, "Maybe we should have."

Maybe indeed, Finn thought grimly. But he said, "No. It's not any of our business what she does."

"Is, too," Pansy insisted. "Izzy's our friend."

Finn grunted, then started up the steps. "Well, our friend will come back when she da—darned well pleases. Come on now, back to bed."

Pansy took one look at him and scampered toward the bedroom like a frightened rabbit. Finn watched her go, then sighed heavily and followed, coming to stand in the doorway and look in on the girls. He could see the outline of two small shapes in his king-size bed. On the far side of the bed, Tansy was curled into a tiny ball, sound asleep. Pansy, on the other hand, lay ramrod stiff with the blanket pulled up to her nose. Her eyes followed Finn warily as he came into the room.

He stood looking down at her for a moment, then he sighed and lowered himself carefully so that he was sitting on the edge of the bed. She scooted toward the middle.

Her lower lip stuck out. "Wish Izzy would come back."

"She will."

"For sure?"

"Yes." She'd damned well better not spend the night at Fletcher's!

"Mommy isn't."

Oh, God. Not this tonight, too. But he supposed they'd have to talk about it sometime. Izzy had told him that the girls had figured out that Meg had abandoned them, but they'd never said anything to him. He supposed they hadn't dared.

Now he ran his tongue over dry lips. "No," he said slowly. "But she made arrangements for you to stay with me."

"You didn't want us." Clearly Pansy could be as blunt as her sister.

"I didn't know you. And I didn't think I wanted any kids." He met her gaze. "Can't a guy change his mind?"

She looked back at him, unblinking. "Have you?"

"Yes."

And he knew it was true even as he said it. He might not be the best substitute parent in the world. God knew he had plenty to learn. But Izzy had got him over the hump. She'd given him a chance to be with them, to get used to them, to find common ground with them. He'd never had much faith in his ability to deal with kids before. He'd been afraid of failing them the way his parents had failed him. But watching her, he'd learned that being there, caring, just being willing to try, was a big part of it.

He wanted to try.

Pansy nodded solemnly. "That's good."

A smiled tipped the corner of Finn's mouth. "We'll make it, the three of us."

"Yes."

He put out his hand and after a moment, she laid her smaller one in it. His fingers closed over it, feeling it warm and trusting in his own. The weight of responsibility settled on him. It wasn't as heavy as he'd feared.

"Maybe," he said, "someday your mother will come back."

Pansy shook her head. "Rather stay with you. And Izzy."

Finn swallowed. "What?"

"I'd rather have Izzy. We didn't mostly see Mommy," Pansy explained. "She was always busy."

Finn could imagine. He nodded.

"Lots of the time we stayed with Izzy and Grandad and Digger and Hewey and Pops," Pansy went on. "I liked that better. But then Grandad died. Me an' Tansy cried."

"I bet."

"Didn't cry when Mommy left."

"Your mother didn't die," Finn said.

"But she's gone. Don't want Izzy to go, too."

Finn sucked in his breath carefully. "Izzy will be back," he promised. "Tonight."

Even if he had to personally track her down in Sam Fletcher's bed and drag her!

But in the future? What about this business of *want to stay here with you and Izzy*? The girls knew she was planning to marry Sam.

But just last night they'd seen Finn kiss her.

His insides seemed to clench. Pansy's fingers tightened around his palm.

"It'll be good," she said sleepily. "Us 'n' you 'n' Izzy." Her eyes fluttered shut, and she rolled over onto her side. In a few minutes she was breathing deeply and evenly. But her fingers stayed wrapped around Finn's.

Us 'n' you 'n' Izzy.

Finn tried not to let himself think about that.

CHAPTER SEVEN

FROM the look of him, when she and Sam brought the girls back to the apartment and dropped them off, Finn wasn't an early evening person, either.

He'd scowled and snarled at her whenever she spoke to him. If he was civil to Sam, it wasn't within her hearing. And when she came downstairs, he'd only glanced at her from where he was messing around in the freezer. But the look he gave her when he saw her in her infamous black dress should have set her hair on fire.

She was glad to get out of the apartment again, eager to be with Sam alone—at last.

He took her to a small Thai restaurant not far from Finn's apartment. It was a quiet, dimly lit place with pale pink damask cloths on the tables and silent waiters who moved to and fro seeing to their every desire. There was soft faintly tinkling music and candlelight and Sam smiling at her across the table.

It was everything her romantic heart had desired.

Except when she wanted them to be looking deeply into each other's eyes and saying the things they hadn't said all day, Sam was talking about the overnight train trip he'd taken between Chiang Mai and Bangkok.

Kiss me, Izzy thought, watching his lips move and taking small sips of *gaeng jued rak bua*, the lotus root soup the waiter had set in front of her.

Sam smiled and reached out a hand and ran it along her fingers as they lay on the table. Ah, she thought. Yes. But then he began talking about the night he'd spent at a famous old colonial hotel in Singapore. Elegant, he said. Memorable.

The waiter brought them *yam pla muk*.

Kiss me, Izzy urged him silently as Sam talked and she picked at the spicy squid salad.

Sam asked about her haircut. "I liked it long," he told her.

"You don't like this?" Her hands went to her hair.

"Sure," he said easily. "I like it however you wear it."

The waiter brought Sam's *gai pad bai krapao* and her *moo tod kratium priktai*. Sam dug into his chicken, not talking at all now.

Kiss me, Izzy begged with her eyes, not even touching her pork.

Sam looked up. "Aren't you hungry? You do like satay, don't you?"

"Yes," Izzy said, poking it with her fork. "Oh, yes." She took a bite.

"I thought so. I remembered the night we went to that little Thai place in the Mission District." He smiled at the memory.

It was the last time he'd been to San Francisco before her grandfather had died. He'd shown up, wholly unexpected as usual, and had spirited her off for the afternoon and evening with her grandfather's blessing.

And he'd asked her to marry him and given her a ring. She'd come home that night radiant, dreaming of a future—with Sam.

"Kiss me," she said.

He stared at her, a spoonful of coconut pudding halfway to his mouth. "What?"

Izzy felt her face burn. She hadn't even realized she'd spoken aloud. "Nothing," she mumbled, ducking her head. "I just wondered if you'd . . . missed me?"

Sam's fingers closed around hers. They played with her newly shaped, perfectly oval, unblemished nails. They caressed the band of the ring he'd given her. His warm brown eyes met hers. "Of course I did. In fact—" and here he gave her a smile to die for "—I think maybe we should go back to my place now and I'll show you just how much."

Izzy felt a tightening in her stomach, a flicker of nerves. Then she smiled, her apprehension easing. His place. He was going to take her to his place. He was finally—at last—going to really kiss her. And possibly do far more than that.

"Yes," she said. "What a good idea."

She wasn't intimidated by the stately marble elegance of his apartment house this time. She had Sam with her, of course. But her hair, her nails, her makeup, her clothes—they all gave her the confidence to feel that she looked as if she belonged.

I do belong, she told herself firmly as they walked past the smilingly obsequious doorman. *I belong with Sam.*

His apartment was on the eighth floor, one of two opening off a quietly elegant foyer. It all looked like something out of *Architectural Digest*—not so much a home as a setting. There were wonderfully thick Persian rugs on the polished oak floors underfoot, colorful Middle Eastern geometric textiles framed on the walls and spread on the backs of a pure white sofa and chairs. Tall teak cabinets contained both sparkling crystal and ornately wrought brass work. And nearly the entire west wall was glass, opening onto a spectacular view of Central Park. To the south she could see the top of the Plaza Hotel and other buildings on Central Park South. Silhouetted against the sunset to the west were the many apartment buildings that lined Central Park West. And almost directly across she could see, twinkling in the trees, the myriad tiny white lights that surrounded the Tavern on the Green.

Home sweet home it was not. Izzy thought back to her grandfather's Victorian to which they'd welcomed Sam whenever he'd come through San Francisco, and she cringed.

But Sam appeared to be making no comparisons. He was smiling at her as she walked toward the windows and stared out. "I used to imagine how you'd look when you saw the view."

Izzy turned toward him. "Awed, that's for sure. I don't know how you get anything done," she said as she looked out over it all. "I'd just stand here and stare."

Sam smiled again and moved toward her. "It is beautiful. But not as beautiful as you."

"It's the new clothes," Izzy said. "The haircut. Did you see my nails?" She waggled them in front of his face. She'd wanted this all night and now she was getting nervous.

"I saw the nails," he said. But he took hold of her hand anyway, drawing her into his arms.

She tried to relax as their bodies touched. *Yes,* she thought. *I want this.* And she waited for the tingling awareness to begin as Sam kissed the back of her neck, her ear, the curve of her jaw. She shivered. But that was all.

"Cold?" He turned her in his arms. "I can warm you up." And then he kissed her the way she'd been hoping to be kissed—with desire, with eagerness, with determination.

And all she could think of was Finn.

No! She squeezed her eyes shut, trying to blot him out. She didn't want Finn! Not here. Not now. *Not ever!*

She kissed Sam back with all the fervor she could muster, all the need she could find.

He groaned and pressed his lips against hers, let his hands slide down her back to cup her buttocks and draw her tight against him so that she felt his arousal. "Let me show you the bedroom," he whispered.

The words were like a blanket of ice. Izzy squirmed, then shook her head, pulling out of his arms, turning back to face the windows. "No, I...not...tonight."

Sam blinked, then stared at her, confused. "Izzy?"

She gave another little shiver and hugged her arms against her breasts. "We can...see it if you want. But all I want to do is look, Sam." She gave him a desperate look. "I'm sorry. I—"

He touched her hair, then gave her a smile. "You're not ready. That's okay. I shouldn't have been so hasty. I should have realized."

How could you, Izzy thought frantically, *when I didn't even realize myself?*

"But you...you're—" She stopped, embarrassed at how aware she was of his arousal.

"I'll live," he said gruffly. "I've lived this long. We'll tour the bedroom another time. Come sit down. Let me get you something to drink."

She should have said no. She should have left while she still had a shred of sanity left. But leaving would have meant going home—back to Finn's.

And she couldn't. Not yet.

So she smothered her guilty feelings and let Sam put a soft instrumental CD on the stereo, then pour her a tiny glass of an orange liqueur. She sipped it, felt her mouth, then her throat tingle and warm. The way her whole body had last night when Finn's tongue had touched hers.

Don't! Don't think about that. Think about Sam. It's Sam you love. Sam you want to marry. She let him lead her to the pure white sofa and draw her down beside him. She let him slip his arm around her, and she allowed herself to settle back against him, to breathe deeply and try to recapture the sense of rightness she always felt around Sam.

"Sam's a good 'un," her grandfather had always said. "I'm glad you've got Sam."

"Yes," Izzy said now.

"I thought you were saying no tonight?" Sam's amused voice said right next to her ear.

She turned, startled, and looked into his deep brown eyes. She gave a faint, desperate shake of her head. "I don't know what I'm saying," she told him in all honesty.

He laughed. "I love you, Iz." And he mussed her hair, then kissed her again.

It was just past one in the morning, when she was sure that Finn would be asleep, that she dared to have Sam take her back to his apartment.

She slipped off her shoes and eased open the door, grateful that it didn't squeak. He had left a light on over the sink in the kitchen, but the first thing she did was glance toward the daybed at the other end of the long room in hopes of seeing his sleeping form lying there.

"About time," Finn's voice growled. He was lounging, slumped against the pillows.

Izzy swallowed. Her fingers tightened on her shoes and she pressed her back against the door. "You didn't have to wait up," she said with a trace of belligerence.

"Didn't I?" His voice was rough, angry almost. "Who else was going to hold Pansy's hand while she fretted and stewed, worried sick because you weren't here?"

Her belligerence fled. "Oh, dear. I'm sorry. I didn't think—"

"No, you damned well didn't!" Finn rose from the bed and came toward her. He was shirtless and barefoot, wearing only a pair of jeans. The low-slung denim trousers somehow only served to heighten her awareness of his masculinity.

She took a nervous step backward. "I'll just go check on them," she said, trying to edge around him.

But Finn caught her arm. "They're all right now. Pansy drifted off about an hour ago."

He wasn't letting go. "I'm...sorry she bothered you," Izzy said.

"Why? They don't matter to you."

"How can you say that?"

"If they did, you'd have been back hours ago. It's damn near two in the morning!" His fingers bit into her arm briefly, then he let go, but stood glowering at her.

Izzy glanced at her watch. "It's five minutes past one. And you could always have called me if she was worried. I left Sam's phone number by the telephone."

"I'll bet Lover Boy would've been thrilled by that. And I've always wanted to get people out of bed! Especially when I'm damn sure they're not sleeping!"

Izzy's cheeks burned, but she certainly wasn't going to deny his accusations. Let him think whatever he wanted. "You could have called," she repeated.

"I managed," he said gruffly.

And she heard a quiet steadiness in his tone that told her more than his words did that he had probably managed very well indeed. She was glad and, unaccountably, found that she regretted not being here to see it.

"Actually I'm not surprised," she said. "I always thought you could."

"Nice of you to have such faith in me," he said sarcastically.

He really did want to pick a fight, and Izzy was fairly certain that pointing it out this time wouldn't diffuse the situation. She started to ease her way past. She'd made it almost to the stairs when his voice stopped her.

"How was your date?" He put a bitter twist on the last word.

Izzy ignored it. "We went to a lovely little Thai restaurant on Amsterdam. I had this great pork dish. Sam had chicken. And then we went back to his apartment and listened to some CDs and—"

"You don't have to give me the play by play."

"Fine," she said, nettled. "I won't." She started up the steps.

"Glad you had such a dandy time," Finn said sourly to her back. "Are you going to be available to watch the girls tomorrow, or are you moving out?"

For her own satisfaction, Izzy would have liked to say she was moving out. But she had to admit, "Not yet. Besides, I promised I'd help take care of them until you got a nanny."

His mouth twisted. "And you, of course, always keep your promises."

Izzy nodded. "I try."

Finn grunted, still obviously dissatisfied. Finally he gave her a curt nod and went into the kitchen to turn off the light. "Good night."

The dismissal was so clear that Izzy felt like a naughty child banished to her room. She didn't move, watching as he stalked across the room to the daybed, totally ignoring her now.

"Want me to kiss you good-night?" He turned, his gaze mocking.

God forbid.

*   *   *

She wanted to go right to sleep. She wanted to dream of Sam.

She lay awake and thought about Finn MacCauley.

It wasn't fair. Sam was the man she loved—the man she'd wanted to marry since the first weekend she'd met him. Sam was kind, loving, fun, gentle. She had known it then; nothing he'd done tonight had changed her mind. He was exactly the way she remembered him.

But she wasn't.

She couldn't get Finn out of her head.

So he was a good kisser, she told herself angrily. So what? That didn't mean anything. Lots of men were good kissers.

But it was more than that, and Izzy knew it. She'd had little respect for Finn when she'd first met him, considering him not much better than his sister. He'd changed her view. There was a sense of purpose about him, a deep core of responsibility that she'd just begun to appreciate. He was brusque, irritable, sometimes gruff, often outspoken. He hadn't wanted the girls and he'd made no bones about it.

But when the alternative was to give them up, to simply shrug and say, "I don't want the responsibility," the way Meg had—the way a lot of people would—he dug down inside himself and found what it took to connect to them. Even to love them.

She could see it in the way he looked at them, in the way he talked to them. She'd heard it in his voice tonight.

And he was a good kisser.

"Oh, damn," Izzy said into her pillow. "Oh, damn."

The girls wanted to go to the beach again.

"It's Sunday," Finn argued. "All five boroughs of New York City will be at the beach on Sunday."

"But it's hot," Tansy wailed.

"Very hot," Pansy said in softer tones, but no less firmly.

Izzy was trying not to take sides. She was cutting up grapefruit sections for breakfast, staying out of Finn's way, wishing she had a good alternative to offer.

The phone rang. Finn held the receiver out to Izzy. "Guess who."

She didn't have to. She took the phone gratefully. "Hi, Sam."

"Sleep well?" he asked her.

"Oh, yes," she said, which was a lie, but she wasn't telling him that. "Wonderful. I want to thank you again for last night."

Finn slapped his coffee mug down so hard the liquid sloshed across the table. Izzy deliberately looked away, leaving it for the twins to fetch him a dishrag to mop it up with.

"My pleasure," Sam said. "What would you like to do today?"

"Oh—" Izzy fumbled "—well, actually, I promised I'd do something with the girls today."

"Again?" Sam didn't sound angry, just bewildered.

"I told Finn I'd help him keep an eye on them," she explained. "He hasn't found a nanny yet."

"My mother could find one," Sam said. "She knows everyone who knows anyone in the city. She's out in East Hampton for the week, but when she gets back—" He stopped suddenly, then said, "How about if we take the girls out for the day? In fact we can stay over and come back tomorrow. It's a huge house right on the beach. They'd love it."

"Stay over? A house on the beach?" Izzy flicked a gaze in the girls' direction. They were eating cereal at the table, but their eyes were fastened on her. At the word *beach* both sets of eyes widened hopefully. "Your mother wouldn't mind?"

"She'll be delighted. What do you say?"

"I'll ask the girls." She turned to them and relayed Sam's suggestion. Both of them beamed.

Then Tansy looked at her uncle, who was wringing out the rag into the sink, his back to them. "Only if Uncle Finn can come, too," she said.

Izzy saw his shoulders stiffen. Her own went rigid. He didn't turn around. She ran her tongue over her lips. "Girls, I don't know..."

"He's a great swimmer. An' you're always sayin' we should spend time with him."

Still Izzy hesitated. She waited, hoping Finn would say he couldn't. He didn't say a word. "Sam, uh," she said finally, "would it be all right if... Finn came, too? The girls would like it," she added quickly, in case he thought it was her idea.

There was a second's indecision on Sam's part, then, "It's a big house. Why not?"

Izzy looked at Finn's back. "Sam says you're welcome to come."

He turned around slowly. His gaze fixed for a moment on her, then went to the girls. They looked at him beseechingly. Finally he looked back at Izzy, then his gaze dropped. His eyes became hooded, his expression unreadable.

Finally he nodded. "All right."

It was a huge house, and in its low-slung, modern, rambling way, just as intimidating as his Fifth Avenue apartment was. So was Sam's mother.

Of course Izzy had seen Mrs. Fletcher the night she'd first gone to Sam's apartment. But then she'd only had a brief glimpse of the elegant woman. This time she met

Amelia Fletcher face-to-face, was subjected to a cool, assessing perusal and was even more grateful for Finn's makeover attempt. Her instincts had been right; the old Isobel Rule would never have passed muster.

This one seemed to. The perusal probably didn't last as long as Izzy thought it did. And then a smile lit Mrs. Fletcher's face and she gave Izzy a kiss on the cheek and a welcoming hug. "At last, my dear. Sam has told me so many wonderful things about you."

I wish he'd told me anything at all about you, Izzy thought rather desperately. She said, "Good old Sam."

"And you've brought friends. How nice."

Izzy introduced them, hoping that Finn wouldn't be horrible. He hadn't said more than fifteen words on the drive out—not to her and Sam, at least. Izzy had offered to let him sit in front with Sam where he could stretch his long legs. But he'd declined.

"We'll be fine back here," he'd said, getting into the back of Sam's Lincoln with the girls. He hadn't said much else, except to the girls. He'd pointed out places as they'd passed them on the Long Island Expressway. He'd told them stories about the Dutch settlers in the seventeenth and eighteenth centuries. Izzy had strained to hear what he was saying, but he made no attempt to pitch his voice so that she and Sam could hear. She crossed her fingers now.

She needn't have worried. Finn was every bit the gentleman when introduced to Amelia Fletcher.

"Actually," he told her, "I believe we met at Maggie Donnelson's dinner party last year."

"Why, so we did! You were the man with that tall gorgeous woman," Amelia recollected. His credentials confirmed, she beamed at him.

"Tawnee Davis," he concurred.

The Rapunzel in the office mural, Izzy remembered. The one with more curves and less clothes than any woman Izzy had ever seen. Clearly Amelia didn't know that.

"How nice that you've been looking out for Isobel."

Finn slanted Izzy a tiny, slightly mocking smile. "Wanted to keep her in one piece for Sam," he drawled.

Amelia smiled and put her hand on his arm, drawing him through the living room and toward the expanse of glass doors that gave way onto the beach. "She's fortunate to have such good friends. And you're the uncle of these two lovely little girls?" She bestowed a smile on Tansy and Pansy. "Come along, girls. I bet you'd like to go for a swim."

Tansy and Pansy went along. So did Finn. He could hardly do otherwise with Amelia gripping him by the arm.

Izzy was left alone with Sam. The minute his mother had Finn and the girls on the other side of the doors, he reached for her, drawing her into his arms. "I missed you," he said, his lips against hers, tasting, nibbling.

Izzy stiffened, then forced herself to relax, to return the nibbles, the kisses. "It was so nice of you to invite the girls along. And Finn, too, of course."

"I wasn't thrilled at the idea, but then I thought, why not? He'll keep them busy better than my mother will." He kissed her again. Harder.

"Your mother said to take the girls upstairs so they could get their swimsuits on." Finn's hard, flat voice cut into the kiss.

Izzy jumped back and spun around to see him standing perhaps ten feet away. He had a girl on either side of him. They were staring openmouthed at her and Sam.

Sam cleared his throat. "Of course. I'll show you." He gave Izzy's hand a squeeze. "I'll show you your room, too."

It was next to his, a cozy Laura Ashley counterpart to his with its English hunting lodge look. The girls' room, with French provincial furniture and thick peach-colored carpet, was down the hall on the far side. Finn's room was even beyond theirs.

"I won't be staying," Finn said. "I have to catch a train back tonight." And when they both looked at him, surprised, he said bluntly, "I have a shoot in the morning. Some of us are working stiffs."

Sam flushed slightly. "I've been working night and day for the last two and a half weeks," he said unnecessarily.

"Of course you have," Izzy put in quickly. "And I'm working right now, if you'll recall," she added, casting a glance back toward the bedroom where the girls were changing into their swimsuits. "While you're back in the city tomorrow," she told Finn, "I think you might want to ask Mrs. Strong to check those agencies and see if they have any new nanny candidates."

Sam snapped his fingers. "Don't forget to ask Mother."

Izzy didn't imagine that Amelia Fletcher would have the faintest idea about procuring a nanny. But Sam knew his mother's capabilities better than she did.

"Doro Milbank's daughter, Eliza, just found a wonderful Iowa farm girl," Amelia said when Sam brought the subject up. They were sitting on lounge chairs overlooking the beach. Izzy was wearing a one-piece maillot in a deep blue color, specially chosen by Anita to bring out her eyes.

It seemed to be bringing out Sam's eyes and Finn's if the way they were watching her was anything to go by.

Izzy, who had never before been self-conscious in a bathing suit, was now. She tried hard to concentrate on what Amelia was saying.

"I'll give Doro a ring," Sam's mother said now, and reached for the portable phone on the small wrought-iron table.

What Finn thought of having Sam's mother seeking a nanny for him wasn't immediately obvious. He was sprawled on a chaise longue, and, after giving Izzy a long appraising look when she first came out, he tipped his dark glasses down. Now his expression was hidden behind them.

Izzy wished she had a pair because she found herself annoyingly interested in looking at him.

It was ridiculous. She'd seen Finn MacCauley's bare chest before. She'd seen him in shorts. But somehow, seeing so much of him so blatantly bare was doing odd things to her insides.

Deliberately she made herself focus on Sam. But somehow Sam, equally bare, held less mystery. Her eyes strayed back.

"I think I'll go swim with the girls," she said and jumped up and ran down to the water without looking back. It was a brisk, breezy day. The waves were fairly large and beyond them she could even see whitecaps. But it didn't deter her.

A good dunking was what she needed. A bracing splash of icy water to dampen her wandering mind. At least she dared hope it would, as she ran past the girls and plunged beneath an incoming wave, relishing the shock of the cold water, then stood and shook her hair back away from her face.

Then, because it really hadn't done much at all, she struck out swimming, plunging beneath each wave, one after another, until at last she was out beyond the breakers. Treading water she turned and looked back.

She was surprised and a little dismayed at how far she'd come. She couldn't see the girls on the shore at all; they were hidden by the breakers as they rolled in. Up the beach she could see the house and Sam and his mother on the deck. At least she thought it was Sam and his mother. They were really too far away to tell. Except they were standing up, looking out to sea.

For her?

The swell of a wave obscured them momentarily from view, then it curled and broke and surfacing just this side of it was a sleek, dark head.

Finn.

His gaze fastened on her. "Swimming to Bermuda?"

"Of course not."

"Could've fooled me. And Lover Boy."

"His name is Sam." Izzy tried to swim away from him, but his long, lazy strokes allowed him to stay abreast of her. "Why are you being so hateful to him? You weren't hateful before!"

"I'm not being hateful." His blue eyes glittered. Maybe it wasn't hate, but she didn't know what it was. He scowled briefly, then gave her a wry look. "Oh, hell, I don't know, maybe I am. He was worried about you. Thought you might drown out here."

"So he sent you after me?"

Finn shrugged. "He had a phone call." He jerked his head toward shore. "Come on. No sense hanging around out here waiting for the sharks to feed."

Izzy's eyes widened. She very nearly sank. *"Sharks?"*

"How should I know? I've never been out here before." He started back toward shore, not waiting for her.

Izzy did a rapid breaststroke after him. "I would have thought you'd be out here all the time, you and Tawnee Davis and all your other fast-lane friends."

He flicked her a glance over his shoulder. "Jealous?"

"No!"

He grinned. "That's what they all say."

"You are hateful," Izzy told his back.

He just laughed and kept swimming, glancing over his shoulder to check the waves. "Do you know how to body surf?"

She nodded.

"I think this is ours."

Izzy, glancing back, saw what he meant. She began stroking faster, trying to catch up to him, to get in front when the wave began to curl. And then she was, and it did, and she felt the surge of powerful water catch her, lifting her forward, then dropping her, flinging her sideways, rushing her along. Finn's body, caught too, angled into hers. They hit, tangled, grappled. Izzy felt what must have been an elbow in her stomach. She gasped, got more than a mouthful of seawater, choked and tried to battle to the surface.

Finn got his footing first and grabbed her, hauling her up into sweet, blessed air. She coughed, choked. He braced her, holding her between his legs. "Are you okay?"

She tried to nod. She kept coughing. The next incoming wave rocked her into his chest. "F-fine."

"I didn't mean to hit you." He put his arms around her and her head was pressed against his chest. She could feel the beat of his heart. Its strong, quick rhythm helped to steady ground her. She felt something else, too. Lower down. Hard and insistent. She lifted her gaze and met his.

A muscle ticked in his jaw. Then he raised his eyes and looked beyond her up toward the beach. "Here comes your savior," he said gruffly, turning her loose.

She turned to see Sam, running down the beach toward them.

Finn stepped away and turned seaward again. "I'll leave you to him."

CHAPTER EIGHT

HE COULDN'T tell himself she hadn't noticed. It was obvious from the stunned expression in her big green eyes that she had. Well, hell, what did she expect?

He was only human. He had needs, desires. Hormones, damn it.

And hanging around watching Sam mooning over Izzy and Izzy looking starry-eyed at Sam wasn't doing a damn thing for them—excepting frustrating him.

He was glad the girls were having a good time, because he sure wasn't. He could hardly wait until it was time to catch the train. Not that he felt much better about leaving them there overnight. Who knew what Sam and Izzy would be doing once Amelia and the girls had gone to bed?

Who knew?

He did, damn it. He knew exactly what he'd be doing if he was engaged to Izzy!

"You're sure you want to stay?" he said to Izzy when they all drove him to the train at six.

"Of course." She gave him a quick smile, but she didn't really meet his gaze. "As long as the girls do." She did look at them. They nodded eagerly. He scowled.

"But we wish you could stay, too, Uncle Finn," Tansy said.

"I'll take good care of them," Sam told him cheerfully. He looped his arm over Izzy's shoulders possessively and drew her against him.

It wasn't what Finn wanted to hear.

He made the best of it, told himself he'd enjoy the break—be glad for a little peace and quiet. Heaven knew he hadn't had any since the day Izzy and the girls had dropped into his life.

But his apartment seemed too big now, too silent. He got home at shortly past midnight, dropped his gear inside the door and went to get himself a beer. As he crossed the room, his footsteps echoed on the hardwood floor.

He downed the beer in two swallows and snagged another. It would help him sleep, he told himself. Not that he wasn't tired.

But once he'd taken a shower, he wandered into the master bedroom. Master, ha. It was definitely the girls' bedroom now. Their clothes and toys had taken over.

He supposed he ought to think about selling the king-size bed and getting a pair of bunks. He could move into the little bedroom once Izzy went to Sam's. He didn't like the hard lump he felt in his gut at the thought. He made himself think about the nanny he was going to have to find. He wasn't going to count on Amelia Fletcher's connections no matter what Sam said.

If he got a live-in girl, he would have to start looking for a different apartment altogether—one with three bedrooms.

He padded down the hall to the room Izzy used. She hadn't closed the blinds and there was enough light from the windows of the high-rise building at the end of the block so he could look around. He hadn't been in here since the day he'd ditched those nude photos of Tawnee in the closet. They'd been her idea, even though he certainly hadn't been unwilling. She was a stunning woman—and definitely steamy enough to make a man's blood run thick and hot.

He pulled open the door now. The photos were still there. He could see them behind Izzy's new clothes. It was too much to hope that she hadn't taken a look. He wondered what she'd thought.

Finn felt an unwelcome warmth in his face. He shut the door and turned away.

A short row of brand-new cosmetics and lotions lined the top of her dresser. Next to it was a small framed picture.

Of Sam, no doubt. Though probably not Sam in the nude. He picked it up, tilting it so he could see it in the light from the window. He saw, not Sam, but an old man he didn't know. He had no trouble guessing who it was.

There was something of Izzy in the old man's grin. There was a mischievous look in his eyes, too—a look Finn had seen on Izzy often enough.

Would Izzy look like him when she grew old? What would Izzy be like fifty or sixty years from now? Finn rubbed his thumb over the picture. He drew a long breath, then carefully, slowly, he looked away, setting the picture back down.

The room was neat as a pin except for something wadded up in the rocker in the far corner. It was Izzy's baggiest, most wretched-looking sweatshirt. Finn picked it up, crushing it in his fingers, rubbing his cheek against the soft thick cotton. It smelled like her—that faint, tantalizing smell of spice and flowers that he'd come to realize meant Izzy was near.

But Izzy wasn't near. Izzy was in East Hampton.

With Sam.

He practically pounced on them the following night when they got home. They were barely halfway up the stairs when he came onto the landing to glare down at them.

He told himself he was worried because there was a storm coming.

For almost an hour he'd been able to hear thunder in the distance and to see reflections of lightning flickering in the sky. Then, finally, above the thunder, he heard voices in the stairwell, girlish voices, and then one far more womanly.

He flung open the door. "It's about time," he fumed. He stomped down to grab the duffel Izzy was carrying, then eased past her, careful not to touch, and took the girls' things, as well. They gave him tired grateful smiles.

Izzy stopped inside the door and waited for him. "Another curfew?" she said, her mildness a rebuke to his irritation.

"I was worried about the girls." He wasn't going to mention having been envisioning Izzy's own body smashed and bloody on the damned highway.

"There were lots of people coming back to the city. It was like a surge of lemmings. We got a late start."

"Where's Lover Boy? Did he drop you at the corner?" He knew he was being a jerk. He couldn't help it.

Izzy's eyes widened at his tone, but hers remained even. "I told him not to come up. He has some work to get done before a meeting tomorrow morning."

"Goody for him." Finn kicked the door shut.

"You're in a jolly mood."

He headed toward the stairs with their bags. "I've got things on my mind. I didn't need to be worrying about them." *About you.*

"You needn't have," she said shortly. "They were in good hands and you know it."

Finn grunted. He slung the girls' bags onto their bed, then carried Izzy's down the short hallway to her room and dropped it inside the door. His gaze flicked toward the bed for just an instant, then he looked away.

He didn't want to remember waking up there this morning, alone—with Izzy's ratty old sweatshirt in his arms.

"I have to be out of town tomorrow," he said abruptly. "I'm doing a location shoot in Bucks County. I trust that won't cramp your style?"

"No problem." Izzy slipped past him into the room. She went to the window and shut it against the rain that had just begun. "I didn't think I left that open," she remarked, then went on, "we'll be fine."

Finn grunted a reply. Damn, why hadn't he remembered to shut the window?

"I have the names of three girls that Sam's mother gave me." Izzy said, looking over her shoulder at him. "I'll give them a call and do a preliminary interview while you're gone. How does that sound?"

It sounded like she could barely wait to get out of his clutches. "Whatever you want." He turned on his heel and stalked down the hall, going to bang on the bathroom door where the twins were running bathwater and giggling. "Come on, ladies, hurry it up in there. You need to get to bed sometime tonight!"

Izzy had arousal on her mind. Her arousal.

And Finn's.

She wasn't such an innocent that she didn't know arousal when she'd felt it pressed hard against her yesterday afternoon on the beach. But, by the same token, she wasn't so naive that she thought it had anything to do with her in particular. And thank God for that.

She was, after all, engaged to Sam! No, it was simply a matter of proximity and the heat of the moment. Finn certainly wasn't in love with her. Sometimes she didn't even think he liked her very much!

She wasn't sure exactly what she felt about him. She sighed and folded her arms beneath her head, giving up on trying to sleep for the present. The rain had stopped, the earlier storm had gone, but once more she could see a flicker of white light in the western sky. A new storm was already on its way. But it was nothing compared to the turbulence she felt within. It was well past midnight and her mind still hadn't stopped plaguing her with memories of how Finn's body had felt pressed against hers.

She had spent all last evening and all today concentrating on Sam—talking to Sam, laughing with Sam, swimming and walking with Sam.

And yet somehow while focusing on Sam, she'd been aware of how like her uncle Finn's Tansy's grin was, and how like her uncle's was Pansy's thoughtful frown.

She'd tried not to think about him. He was safely back in the city, doing his job—and she was where she ought to be. She had no business thinking about another man, no business watching his every move, and no business at all permitting her body to respond to the excitement she perceived in his!

It would be all for the best if one of the girls Amelia's friend recommended was able to take on the girls. Soon.

Finn seemed in no hurry to move things along, but she was. And why should he be when he'd done his part? No, it was up to her. She would start making calls first thing in the morning. Tansy and Pansy needed to be getting settled into their new life.

And goodness knew, Izzy needed to be getting on with hers.

At least the two days in East Hampton had been a success. Amelia Fletcher wasn't nearly as intimidating up close as she had been when Izzy had glimpsed her the first time. Still she was all that was elegant and refined, no doubt about that; so Izzy was glad she'd agreed to Finn's deal. Her new haircut and clothes, which Amelia had taken for granted, had definitely eased her acceptance into Sam's world. She supposed that Amelia might have welcomed her as a daughter-in-law-to-be anyway, but Izzy was glad she hadn't put it to the test. She wanted to make life easier for Sam, not harder.

Sam.

Dear, sweet lovable Sam.

How easy he was to please. How undemanding. How unlike Finn MacCauley.

And there she was, thinking about him again!

Izzy pounded her pillow. She rolled over and shut her eyes—and saw for the thousandth time the wave she'd caught with Finn, felt once more the press of his body against hers.

Damn it! She leapt out of bed and went to stand at the window, opening it and taking great lungsful of humid, sticky city air. It was a measure of the content of her thoughts that she considered the air purer than the desires buffeting her body.

A movement on the terrace below caught her attention.

Finn, with his back to her and his hands braced on the flower boxes that lined the perimeter, stood staring up at the sky. His head was tipped back, his dark hair a swath of midnight in the flickers of lightning. All he wore was a pair of low-slung jeans and she could just make out the strong column of his spine and the breadth of his bare shoulders. He looked untamed, wild. Like a wolf in a clearing even though he stood in the middle of one of the biggest cities in the world.

Izzy's fingers tightened on the window ledge. She didn't move, just looked. All at once a sharp flash of lightning chopped through the sky, startling her. "Oh!"

Finn jerked, then turned and looked up.

Their gazes met, locked. His jaw was tight, his expression stark. His chest rose and fell quickly, his whole body seemed poised to move, to reach for her. He didn't.

She only wished he would.

Frantic at the direction of her thoughts, Izzy pulled back and slammed the window shut.

He was gone when she got up. She didn't know if he'd left early because he had to travel to Pennsylvania or if he simply needed to get away. She didn't question it. She was only relieved.

"When's he coming back?" Pansy asked.

"Tonight, I imagine," Izzy said, pouring them bowls of breakfast cereal. Hours from now. But even if it was days, it wouldn't be long enough.

As soon as they'd finished eating, she called the names on the list Amelia had given her. The first girl had already taken a job the previous week. The second agreed to come and talk to them later that morning. The last would come in the afternoon.

"Do we have to pick one of them?" Tansy asked Izzy worriedly.

"Not if you don't like them."

"We won't," both girls said flatly.

"You might." She dared to hope.

"Not as good as you. Why can't you stay?" Pansy asked.

"Because of Sam, you know that. And—"

"You don't got to marry Sam," Tansy said. "You could marry Uncle Finn. You kissed him."

"It...was a mistake." Izzy felt her face burn. "Besides, he doesn't want to marry me. We're not in love with each other. You marry the person you love," she said firmly.

"Does Mommy love Roger?"

"I think she must," she said carefully. "Otherwise she wouldn't have gone with him, would she?"

"Guess not. But Uncle Finn said she loves us, too," Pansy said. "Even though she left us."

"Because she wanted what was best for you. And she thought that would be living with your uncle Finn."

"Be best yet if we lived with you, too," Tansy said stubbornly.

"I'm sure there is a lovely girl looking for a nanny job who will be just right for you, too."

"Maybe," Tansy said dubiously.

"Doubt it," Pansy said under her breath.

But the first girl who arrived surprised them both. Her name was Rorie. She had grown up in a small town in Oklahoma, and though she'd been in the city for two years, she still had a bright, fresh enthusiasm and a country-bred openness that immediately caught both Tansy and Pansy's attention, not to mention Izzy's.

Best of all, she'd been a lifeguard at the local swimming pool in high school, so she shared Tansy's zeal for the water, and she liked to draw. Her last job had ended when the family she was working for had gone abroad for three years. She needed to find something soon, she said, or she would be going back to Oklahoma.

"What do you think?" Izzy asked the girls when Rorie had departed.

"She's okay," Tansy said cautiously, but she didn't look as doubtful as she sounded.

"Maybe," Pansy agreed. "But I'd still rather have you."

The second girl didn't hold a candle to Rorie.

"She'd have been more interesting with a ring in her nose," Tansy offered after she left. Pansy didn't say anything at all.

"So shall we ask your uncle to interview Rorie?" Izzy pressed.

They shrugged. "Guess so."

Izzy hoped Finn would like Rorie. She wouldn't feel bad about leaving the girls with her. She'd miss them. But she could come and see them. They could spend weekends with her and Sam sometimes, give Finn a break, let him take out one of his jet-setting girl friends. That was a good idea, wasn't it?

When she asked Sam about it that evening when he came to take them out to dinner, he said, "Sure. Don't see why not."

So everything was fine. Perfect. Rorie would come. Izzy could go. Sam would be happy. So would Finn. So would she. It would all work out to everyone's best advantage. So why, knowing this, did Izzy feel so unsettled? So irritable? Why was her stomach twisting? Why were her hands clenching into fists?

Because Finn was so late getting home, that was all.

It was past ten and there was still no sign of him. She and Sam had put the girls to bed, then they'd adjourned downstairs to sit on the sofa beneath Finn's huge wildlife photos and listen to CDs. Sam had put on something soft and instrumental. Romantic. He'd drawn her into his arms and nuzzled her cheek.

"How about a cup of coffee?" Izzy said, twisting away.

"No, thanks." Sam drew her closer, snuggling her in the curve of his arm. His lips brushed her temple. She could feel his breath against her cheek.

"Tea?" she suggested. "I'm thirsty." She slipped out of his grasp and shot to her feet, heading for the kitchen.

Sam hauled himself up and followed her. She filled the kettle, set it on the burner, wiped up a nonexistent spill, straightened the towel on the rack. Sam leaned against the refrigerator, watching her. The soft moody sound of a saxophone drifted through the room. Izzy got a cup down out of the cupboard and turned to Sam. "Sure you won't have one?"

He sighed. "All right."

She made the tea. They carried it back into the living area and sat down on the sofa. Sam sat at one end. Izzy sat at the other. He moved closer. She had nowhere to go.

They drank their tea. Sam watched her. She looked at him, then away. When they finished at last, Izzy still hung onto her cup, carrying it to her lips every few minutes, hiding behind it, avoiding the hungry look in Sam's eyes. Finally he reached out and took the cup from her, setting it on the table. Then he leaned forward and touched his lips to hers. Izzy held absolutely still. Didn't move. Didn't even breathe.

Sam came closer, raised his arms and slipped them around her. His lips still clung to hers. His eyes started to close. Izzy's flew open at the sound of footsteps on the stairs. She leapt to her feet, knocking Sam away. "He's coming!"

Sam, rocked back, looked at her, befuddled. "Who?"

"Finn!"

"So?" He reached for her hand. "I doubt if he'd be shocked. I think he's seen people kiss before."

Izzy shook him off. "I know that." She folded her arms across her breasts. "I just...don't want him walking in on us."

Sam looked like he might have protested, but the door opened. Finn came in. He looked first at Sam on the sofa, then at Izzy, who was heading for the kitchen with the teacups in her hands. He didn't say anything.

"Water's almost hot. I can reheat it in just a minute if you want some tea?" Izzy said brightly.

Finn looked at Sam, who was raking his fingers through his hair and scowling.

"How about you, Sam? Another cup?" Izzy went on, moving to turn on the kettle again.

"It isn't tea I want right now," Sam said flatly, his eyes fastened on her.

There was no question at all what he did want. Izzy could see that from the look in them. She knew Finn saw it, too. She went red.

"I found the perfect girl for you. Nanny, I mean," she said to Finn. "The twins like her a lot already. She's the answer to your prayers."

Finn didn't say a word. A muscle ticked in his cheek.

"Her name is Rorie. She's from Oklahoma. She swims. She was a lifeguard, in fact. And she draws and paints. I set up an interview for you at the end of the week." She was babbling, but she couldn't help it.

"Cancel it."

"What? Why?" Izzy stared at him.

"I have a shoot out of town starting Thursday. For a week. In Jackson Hole, Wyoming."

"A week? In Jackson Hole?" Izzy digested that. "No problem. Is there, Sam?" she said brightly. "You don't mind if I stay one more week, do you? You can even help me."

"No," Finn said before Sam could open his mouth.

Izzy stared. "What do you mean, no? Of course he can. He's wonderful with the girls."

Finn shrugged, as if it didn't matter. "You're not staying here. You're all coming with me."

CHAPTER NINE

SHE should have said no.

She should have firmly, flatly, definitely turned Finn down. She should have said that under no circumstances was she going to go traipsing off to Wyoming with him and the girls, leaving Sam—her fiancé, for goodness sake—behind when she'd waited so long for them to be together.

But the word hadn't come.

She'd stood there, openmouthed and astonished, and let him bulldoze her into it.

She was a fool.

She told herself that time and again over the next three days. But she didn't back out. The only thing she did manage was to get him to agree to interview Rorie before they left.

She was hired—for when they got back, he said flatly. Not before.

Thursday morning bright and early, she and Finn and the girls got on a plane.

It was only for a week, Izzy rationalized. It would be easier on the girls if she was there. She could talk to them about how to make things go well with Rorie. She could give them advice on dealing with their cranky uncle—as if she knew!

She could spend one last week with Finn.

It was there, in the back of her mind. Unvoiced. Unacknowledged. Unwise in the extreme. But Izzy couldn't help that.

Maybe it would help her get over him. Give her such a dose of Finn MacCauley that she would go off him for good.

She dared to hope.

But then, she was a fool.

In her naïveté, Izzy had supposed that Jackson Hole would be set in a sort of deep narrow hole surrounded by mountains. She got the mountain part right, but the town was in fact in a rather broad flat valley with the Tetons on one side and another less imposing-looking range of mountains on the other, though the town proper did bump up against a couple of rather steep hills on its edges.

Izzy wouldn't have called it a hole. But whatever else it was, the town was lovely, with its small square surrounded by upscale shops selling everything from finely woven Navajo rugs to moose-shaped cookie cutters to designer original dresses. Its covered boardwalks lent an Old West veneer to its increasingly yuppie core. But Izzy discovered that even though she couldn't afford a lot of what the very exclusive shops had to offer, there was a bit of real working west in Jackson Hole still to be found underneath.

She saw it in the hardware stores where men in dusty jeans bought rolls of baling wire, in the saddle shop where fancy tooled leather rigs were outnumbered by no-nonsense working cowboys' saddles, and in the substantial wholesome food dished up at the mom-and-pop café where she took the girls for lunch the first day while Finn was, in his words, "reconnoitering," looking for suitable locations to take shots for the clothing catalog that had sent him out here.

"I'll meet you at five," he'd promised when he'd dropped them off beside one of the elk antler archways that led into the square.

Izzy started to point out that the reason he'd given for bringing them was so that he could spend time with the girls, but he drove off before she'd had a chance. And it was just as well, anyway. The less time she spent in his company, the better.

She was already committed to a week in a hotel suite with Finn MacCauley.

It didn't bear thinking about.

Of course they'd have the girls with them as they always did. It shouldn't be any different than the weeks she'd spent with him in his apartment. But somehow it was.

Or maybe she was.

Different. More aware. Of Finn.

"—go with him," Tansy said, looking up at her expectantly.

Izzy jerked back to the present, trying desperately to figure out what the little girl had been saying. But there weren't enough clues, and finally she had to ask, "What? I'm sorry. I was thinking about something else."

"I said I hope tomorrow we can go with Uncle Finn when he shoots," Tansy said patiently. "Don't you?"

No, Izzy thought. But she didn't want to explain her reasons to the girls, so she simply smiled and drew their attention away.

They spent most of the afternoon exploring the shops. And when the girls wearied of that, she took them to a playground not far from the center of town where they raced around and jumped off things and pushed each other in the swings. When they were sufficiently winded, she steered them back toward the square. Finn would be there soon. Too soon.

They'd stopped in front of a window with a display of Hopi kachinas in one of the shops when she heard, "There you are," from behind them.

"Uncle Finn!" Tansy gave a gleeful shout. "You're early."

Izzy, who had been preparing herself for five o'clock, didn't have her armor in place and, as she turned around, her heart skipped a beat at the sight of him.

Finn bounded up the steps of the boardwalk toward them, his dark hair wind-tossed, his lean, tan face breaking into a smile at the girls' greetings. There was an energy in him that Izzy had never seen in another man. And when he raised his eyes and met Izzy's, she saw a light in them that drew her like a moth to a flame.

And if you go to him, you'll get well and truly scorched, my girl, she reminded herself firmly. She allowed herself a polite smile, no more.

It didn't do any good. He ruffled the girls' hair, then took Izzy by the arm and led her down the boardwalk. "I've got eight spots picked out," he said, and she heard the eagerness in his voice. "I'd like to tell the models to go hang and just shoot scenery. I saw some elk!" He was like a small boy, his enthusiasm bubbling over.

"You've never seen elk before?"

"I told you, I had a deprived childhood." His tone was light, but beneath it she heard the truth in what he said.

But she simply replied, "Poor you," in the same light tone and reached up to tousle his hair. She thought that would be safe enough, but the feel of the silky strands against her fingers sent a shaft of pure longing through her. She jerked her hand away and tucked it in the pocket of her jeans.

"Can we see elk, Uncle Finn?" Tansy asked him, hopping up and down alongside.

He looked at Izzy, the eager light still shining in his eyes. "Want to?"

"Oh, yes!"

He had been right to bring the girls; Izzy saw that very quickly. The time they were spending together—looking for and finding the elk, then later, after dinner, sitting by the river, watching the sunset over the Tetons, all three of them leaning against the trunk of a tree and each other—was invaluable, bonding them in a way that all their days in New York could never have done.

She stood a little bit apart, watching them, not the sunset, and felt a faint hollow aching deep inside her. As if they were a family and she was not.

Well, heavens, the rational part of her argued, that was only the truth. She *wasn't* their family. She didn't have a family yet. She would, though, soon. With Sam.

She needed to call Sam. He had said to ring when she got here and she hadn't done it yet. She turned and started back.

"Where're you going?" Finn called.

She didn't look back. "I have to call Sam."

He muttered something under his breath and scrambled to his feet. "Come on, girls."

"You don't have to come."

"Yes," he said. "I do."

The damn woman had Sam on the brain. Fletcher was all she ever thought about. How the hell could she spend all her time thinking about him when there were elk to be seen, mountains to be climbed, rivers to be fished?

Not to mention Finn and the girls.

It reminded him all too much of his childhood, when his foster parents had always been far more interested in their own kids than they had been in him. He understood it, even though he resented it. Back then being second best had been a way of life.

It wasn't now. For this week, anyway, Izzy was going to pay attention to him!

So he hung about all the time she was on the phone to Fletcher. He checked his watch and looked impatient—which he was—and eventually she hung up and rejoined him and the girls on the deck of the hotel where they were staying.

"It's getting late," she told them. "Almost nine. And by your internal clocks it's even later since we've gained two hours coming out here."

"But it isn't even really dark yet," Tansy protested.

"It will be by the time you're ready for bed," Izzy said, chivvying them off toward the elevator that would take them to the suite.

It was a two-bedroom suite. The girls had one of them. No comment was made about the other. Finn rather hoped Izzy wouldn't notice until it was too late. There was a king-size bed in the other room, after all. Big as a glacier.

Izzy had taken one look and said, "I'm not sleeping in there with you."

He didn't argue then. And as soon as they had tucked the girls up in bed, Finn had got a call from the catalog executive who wanted to talk to him over drinks down in the bar. He gnashed his teeth, but in the end he'd no choice but to go.

He got back to discover Izzy in a flurry of activity, making up a bed on one of the love seats in front of the television.

"Don't be ridiculous," he said.

She didn't answer, just snapped out a sheet and tucked the end in along one arm of the love seat. Then she spread a blanket on top of it and plumped a pillow at the other end. "There."

"It isn't long enough, even for you."

"It will be fine." She didn't look at him as she spoke, just disappeared into the bedroom with the glacier-size

bed and shut the door. Moments later she was back
wearing, he presumed, her nightgown. She had a robe
on over it, covering her from neck to toe. Finn rolled
his eyes.

Izzy settled herself on the love seat, pulled her knees
up against her chest and wrapped her arms around them.

Finn, watching her, scowled. She didn't look at him.

He didn't move, just stood there. She didn't move,
just sat there. Finally he sighed. "Sweet dreams," he
muttered.

Finn was right: the love seat was at least a foot too short
for her. She told herself it wouldn't matter, that she could
easily curl up and be perfectly comfortable. She was
wrong.

She tossed and turned, muttered and grumbled. She
got a kink in her back, an ache in her neck, and more
time than she wanted to remain aware of Finn MacCauley
in the next room. She got up and paced the small living
room, trying to think of Sam.

She stubbed her toe on the coffee table in the dark
and bit back a yelp.

The door to the bedroom flew open. "What's wrong?"

She hopped up and down, holding her foot. "Nothing.
I tripped."

"You were sleepwalking?"

"I was not sleepwalking!" The second she said it, she
wondered if she might have been better off claiming she
had been.

"Can't sleep, huh?" Finn came closer. The drapes were
lined and cut out most of the light, but she didn't need
to see him to know how close he was. His presence was
almost tangible. She backed away, tumbled over the
damned table again, this time landing on her bottom.

"Oh, for God's sake!" Finn flicked on the light. Izzy tried to scramble up, grabbing for her robe at the same time. Finn snatched it out of her hands and tossed it aside, then put his hands on her arms. "Are you all right?"

"F-fine. Let me go. I'll just go back to bed."

But he didn't let her go. On the contrary, she felt herself being lifted into his arms. "Hold still," he snapped when she started to struggle. And cradling her against his chest, he carried her into the bedroom and set her gently on the bed.

"I don't want—"

"I don't give a damn what you want. You're sleeping here."

"No. I—"

"Yes." And he flipped off the light again, then flung himself onto the bed beside her, one arm going across her, pinning her down.

"Finn!"

"Lie still and stop panicking. You're like a skittish colt. What do you think I'm going to do to you?"

Izzy sucked in a breath. "N-nothing. Are you?"

His body was almost rigid next to hers. "No, damn it, I'm not." But he didn't move his arm away either.

They lay next to each other, breathing hard, not moving at all. Seconds passed. Minutes. The feel of his arm against her breasts made her tremble. She wiggled slightly.

His grip tightened slightly. "Does my arm hurt you?"

"N-no."

"Then shut up and go to sleep."

If she hadn't been able to sleep on the love seat for thinking about him, how on earth was she going to when his body was lying mere inches away?

Izzy eased around onto her side, facing away from him. A mistake. He spooned his body around the curve of hers, his arm tucking beneath her breasts and pulling her back firmly against him.

"I—Sam . . ." she began.

"Screw Sam." Finn snugged her even closer. She could feel his breath against her ear. She held herself rigid, but it was hard to stay rigid for very long, especially since the warmth of his body made her want simply to snuggle back against him. She couldn't resist any longer. Her muscles gave out; her body softened, and without even wanting to, she found herself nestling more deeply into his arms.

"That's better," he growled.

Something soft brushed her ear. His lips? Surely not. But the mere possibility sent a tingle clear through her. She sighed.

And then, against all odds, she slept.

Finn was gone when she awoke. Before she even opened her eyes, she missed the warmth of his body next to her. Instinctively she reached for him—and felt bereft when he wasn't there.

Fool, she called herself and hopped out of bed. There was a note on the dresser. *We're shooting by the river. I'll leave the car. Bring the girls down after you've eaten.*

Imperious, aren't you? Izzy thought. No *would you please* or *if you'd like to.* Just *Bring the girls.*

But maybe he wasn't being imperious, just realistic. She knew quite well that wherever he was the girls would want to be. She wanted to be there, too.

The girls hurried through breakfast.

"He really said we could come?" Tansy demanded.

Izzy showed them the note. "But you've got to stay out of the way. And don't pester."

"We won't," Pansy promised.

"We never pester," Tansy said solemnly.

Izzy rolled her eyes. The girls giggled.

Finn was crouched behind a camera, but he looked up at their approach. "Come here."

The girls scampered over. He reached into the camera bag at his feet and pulled out two small point-and-shoot type cameras, then handed one to each of his nieces.

"You've got to help me out," he told them. "I'm shooting the main shots, but they're planning to use some candid ones as well. I don't have time to do that, too. Nor do I have six hands. So I'm hoping you'll help me out."

The girls stared at him, their eyes like saucers. "Really?" Tansy said.

"They won't use anything that's not good, mind you. But if you get some good shots, well . . . you might be getting your first photo credits."

"Wow," Tansy breathed.

Pansy bit her lip. Izzy could see the doubt written on her face.

Finn must have seen it too. "You don't have to if you don't want to," he said gently.

"I want to," the little girl said stoutly. "It's just . . . I'm not very good."

Finn lifted her chin with his finger so that she looked up to meet his gaze. "You're good enough for me."

Izzy wanted to hug him. Pansy did. And when Finn looked up and met Izzy's gaze with a smile of his own, her heart did a little dance.

"Hurry up, Finn. I'm freezing!" one of the models whined from the canoe, where she sat wearing shorts and a T-shirt and trying to look glamorous and athletic at the same time.

Finn dragged his gaze away from Izzy and went back to work. She felt privileged; she got to spend the rest of the day looking at him.

It was dangerous. Playing with fire. Yet she couldn't seem to stop herself. And it wasn't as if she was *doing* anything with him, for goodness sake! She was just looking. Window-shopping.

After all, she defended herself, they had slept together all night and they hadn't done a thing!

That ought to mean something, oughtn't it?

It didn't mean what she hoped it meant—that she was indifferent. In reality, it meant she was letting her guard down, getting overconfident about her ability to resist him.

She allowed herself to relax and enjoy watching him shoot by the river. She didn't even resist when he waited for her to share the bed with him that night. She cuddled close and savored every moment of those hours she spent in his arms. That night and the next and the night after that.

She wasn't being unfaithful to Sam, she assured herself. She hadn't done anything!

Except give Finn her heart.

There was no denying it, no pretending it wasn't so. It was.

She didn't know precisely when she realized it. Perhaps she'd known it all along. Since she'd come.

Perhaps that was *why* she'd come.

She had spent the week fighting it—pretending she was using the time to get sick of Finn. But all the while she'd been watching him, basking in his attention, snuggling nightly in his arms, she'd only really been doing one thing—lying to herself.

But now, faced with the idea of going back to New York tomorrow—of packing her things and saying goodbye to him, she couldn't lie any longer. She'd fallen in love with him.

What about Sam? Didn't she love Sam?

Once she'd thought she had. Maybe, in a way, she still did—the way a sister loved a brother, the way one friend loved another dearly.

But not the way she loved Finn.

She watched him now, crouched on the riverbank with the girls. He'd spent the week involving them in his life, alternately teasing them and teaching them, becoming slowly but surely for them the father they'd never had.

Was that why she had fallen in love with him? Or was it something more?

She loved watching him work. He saw things in people that no one else saw. Another photographer might simply have tried to make the clothes look good. Finn made the people look good. He encouraged them to have fun, to be themselves—and while they were, he caught their joy.

He caught hers, too, without her even knowing it. She'd thought he was just taking background bits for the catalog and snapshots to put in an album with the girls' efforts to commemorate the trip when they were back home.

Maybe he had. But he'd also taken photos of her.

She found them late that last afternoon. He'd gone back out to take some makeup shots, and had left them on the desk, arranged in an almost haphazard fashion, as if he'd been comparing one Izzy to another. Izzy, not expecting to see any of herself, stared at them, amazed.

He'd caught her dreamy-eyed and wistful one night as she'd sat watching the girls toast marshmallows in a camp fire. He'd caught her breathless and laughing when she'd tipped the canoe and come up soaking wet. He'd captured her pensive and cheerful, serious and silly, smiling and looking as if she'd lost her very best friend.

She knew exactly when he'd taken that last photo. It was the time she'd seen him playing with the girls on the lawn, happy together as a family—and she'd felt her eyes begin to sting and her throat to ache. Finn had glanced up and waved at her to come and join them.

She'd taken half a step, then stopped and shook her head. She'd wanted to—*oh, God, how she had wanted to*—but she had no right. She'd turned blindly away and went to catch the lift to the top of the ski run. There was no skiing in the middle of the summer. But the lift ran anyway, taking tourists high into the Tetons so they could experience the view.

She'd gone to seek that view, to gain some distance, some perspective. She'd seen nothing but the scene playing in her mind. Finn and the girls. A family together—without her.

She didn't remember the tears rolling down her cheeks, but Finn had caught them there. Had he followed her up the mountain? He must have. He'd never said a word.

Had he known what she was thinking? Had he suspected she'd fallen in love with him? She hoped not.

It was the last thing he would want. He'd taken the twins because he had to, and now he'd grown to love them. They were his nieces. She was nothing to him, had no claim on him. He wasn't going to grow to love her.

She didn't want him to. She wanted love, yes. But love that came out of joy, not out of duty.

She wanted the impossible.

Don't, she cautioned herself. *Oh, don't.* But it was too late. She already had.

She set the photos down on the desk again and drew a steadying breath. It wouldn't do to go all weepy. She'd spoil what little time they had left.

It wasn't much. Tomorrow they would be on their way back to New York. The next day Rorie would start work so that Izzy could go to Sam.

She knew now that she wouldn't be going to Sam—except to explain. She'd be going back to San Francisco, older and wiser and in love with a man who would never love her.

But she had today—tonight. She'd better make a few memories to take with her when she went.

He came in when there was scarcely any daylight left. And when he finally returned to the suite, he looked worn out. There were dark circles under his eyes and deep lines bracketing his mouth. Izzy wished she had the right to go to him and rub his shoulders or massage his back.

He barely looked at her. "I'm going to grab a shower."

When he came out twenty minutes later, she expected he'd collapse on the bed and leave her and the girls to fend for themselves. She could take them down to the cafeteria, she supposed. They wouldn't mind.

But he had put on a clean pair of jeans and was buttoning a fresh shirt. He had shaved and his dark hair, damp from the shower, was neatly combed. Still, there was a tight, intense expression on his face, the skin stretched tautly over his cheekbones.

"I'll call room service," he said. "What do you girls want to eat?"

"Room service?" Tansy and Pansy's eyes got wide. "Really?" They pored over the menu and made their decision with little help from Izzy.

"I'll just have soup and a salad," she said when he went to call down the order. She wasn't feeling hungry in the least. But when the order came, her soup and salad weren't on it. Nor was anything for Finn.

"What—" Izzy began, but there came just then a knock on the door.

Finn opened it and ushered one of the models into the room. Izzy's heart fell to her feet. Of course he'd want to go out at least once while he was here. She could hardly expect him to spend every night with her and the girls.

"You know Cathy," he said to Izzy. "She's going to baby-sit tonight."

"What?"

"We're going out." He met her gaze levelly. "Get dressed." His expression was even more intense. There was a glitter in his eyes she'd never seen before.

She ran her tongue over her lips, then looked down at her jeans and T-shirt. They were both products of her shopping expedition with Anita. "I am dressed," she said faintly.

"Your black dress."

Izzy gulped. Finn waited. She went to put on her black dress.

She remembered Anita giggling and saying, "Less is more, you know," when she'd first tried it on. It certainly felt like less tonight. She was extraordinarily conscious of her bare arms and shoulders.

"Sam will think you're a knockout," Anita had promised.

Izzy didn't remember what Sam had thought. She couldn't forget Finn's kiss.

She was insane to be wearing it tonight. It would just remind her of what she was leaving behind—of the man she wanted and couldn't have. She should never have brought it. She wouldn't have, except he'd insisted.

"Take this," he'd said, tossing it into her bag as she was packing.

Had he been planning this?

She could hardly come right out and ask him. Another, more sophisticated woman might have been able to—without blushing. Not Izzy.

At least she had the soft rose-colored wool shawl Anita had chosen to complement the dress—and hide her bare shoulders. It helped, but she would look like an idiot clutching it tightly all night.

"Ready?" Finn called from the living room.

"One second." She took a minute to run a brush through her hair and put on a bit of lipstick. Then she slipped into a pair of low heels and took a deep breath.

He was waiting when she came out. The expression on his face told her that the dress, even with the shawl, was everything he remembered.

"Dynamite dress," Cathy said. "You look gorgeous. You should have been shooting her all week," she said to Finn.

"I was."

Cathy looked at him, nonplussed.

"I don't have a coat with me," Izzy said self-consciously.

"You won't need it." He caught her hand and drew her toward the door. "I'll keep you warm."

It was a damned good thing she had that shawl over her shoulders. Finn didn't figure he could be held responsible for what he might have done if she hadn't. That much creamy skin open to view, just asking to be kissed, was provocation for any man.

And for a man as aware—as aroused—as he had been for the last week, well . . . it didn't bear thinking about.

Finn sucked in his breath harshly. He wished the elevator would hurry up. He didn't like being in such a small space with Izzy. The shawl wasn't cast iron after all—and neither was he. He dropped her hand as soon as the elevator doors shut. Now they stood barely half a foot apart. He tried not to look at her. But the elevator was walled with mirrors. There were Izzys ad infinitum, everywhere he looked.

At last the doors slid open again. He steered her through the lobby toward the parking lot.

"I thought you said we'd be inside."

"We will be. Not here."

"Where?"

"A friend of mine has a house. We're invited there."

He didn't mention that George was summering in France. He simply tucked her into the passenger seat of the rental car and shut the door. He was grateful for the steering wheel to hang onto. It made the fine tremor in his hands less noticeable.

He just hoped he had enough finesse to get them through the meal before he made love to her. At least he'd stopped lying to himself about how badly he wanted to.

He'd thought he was being clever at the beginning of the week, taking her into his bed. And then when she'd actually fallen asleep in his arms, he'd been completely foiled. She'd *trusted* him!

How could he make love to her now?

He paid for his sins. He hadn't slept in days. She thought the dark circles under his eyes were from working too hard. Not a chance.

"Which friend?" she asked. "Have I met him?"

He turned into the gravel lane that wound through an aspen grove toward the house. "His name's George Leland. He's a producer. Spends a lot of his time in Europe."

Which was the whole point. For once Finn wanted to focus entirely on Izzy. He wanted to watch her face light up when she was enchanted, watch her eyes sparkle when she was pleased, watch her lips part when he kissed her...

Whoa. Damn it. He was getting ahead of himself again.

But he'd stopped denying that he wanted her. Desperately. As he'd never wanted another woman. Even if she was engaged.

He'd never in his life plotted to take another man's woman. He wasn't plotting to take Izzy now.

Well, not exactly.

He was simply plotting to show her that she didn't love Sam.

He didn't want her to make a bad marriage and wake up someday soon and find herself tied for life to a man she didn't love.

That was all he was doing. It was perfectly straightforward. And if he had to make love to her to do it— well, a man had to do what a man had to do.

Izzy sat silently, not looking at him, her fingers knotted together in her lap. She didn't make a sound until at last they curved out of the trees along the edge of the slope and the expanse of the valley and the twinkling lights of Teton Village and scattered ranches lay below them.

"Oh, my!" She leaned forward, peering out as they came out of the clearing and the house came into view. A smile curved her mouth. "It's lovely."

He stopped the car next to the house and came around to open the door for her. She was already halfway out. He scowled at her.

She shrugged. "Sorry. But then, you know the real me. I don't have to be Miz Perfect for you." She bounded the rest of the way out.

"No," Finn said hoarsely. "I like you just the way you are."

The color in Izzy's cheeks deepened and she turned abruptly away to gaze out over the valley, focusing on the lights of the village below. "What a spectacular view."

Finn, looking at her, not the lights, could only agree.

"I suppose we should go in. I imagine we're keeping your friend waiting."

There were lights on inside. He'd come up earlier, after the shoot had finished—early for once—and had started the meal. He'd put the wine in to chill and browned the meat and onions, chopped the carrots and started the boeuf bourguignon to simmering. He'd made a salad, put a loaf of French bread in the oven and set the timer to turn the oven on at eight, then set the table, complete with candles ready to be lit. He'd laid wood for a fire and started it going. Only then had he gone back down to the suite where she and the girls were waiting.

Now he slipped George's key out of his pocket and fitted it in the lock.

"What are you—"

He didn't answer, just opened the door and steered her in.

"Where's your friend?"

"Paris."

Izzy stopped dead and stared at him. *"What?"*

Finn shrugged negligently. "He's in Paris. He lent me the house." Brushing past her, he headed for the kitchen to check on the boeuf bourguignon. Lifting the lid, he sniffed, then gave it a stir. "Almost ready. There's a salad in the fridge. Will you put it on the table in the dining room?"

He didn't look to see if she obeyed. He held his breath and tried to act as naturally as possible. Izzy didn't move for another few seconds. Then, finally, she did.

The refrigerator door opened. Izzy carried the salad to the dining room. Finn took the bread out of the oven and set it on the counter, then opened the wine. She didn't come back into the kitchen.

He edged over far enough so that he could glance into the dining room. He didn't see her. Carrying the wine bottle, he went for a more thorough look.

The salad was on the table. Izzy was standing at the far end of the living room, staring down at the burning logs in the fireplace. Hating him for his subterfuge? Missing Sam?

He cleared his throat. She jumped.

"Penny for your thoughts?" he said softly. And they'd better not be about Sam!

Izzy smiled a little tremulously. "I was wondering why you'd bring me here if your friend was in Paris."

"I didn't want to share you with him." He grinned at her.

"Don't say that!" she protested.

"It's true."

But she shook her head and turned away.

Stymied, Finn suggested, "How about a glass of wine?"

Izzy twisted the ends of the shawl. "All right."

He poured two, handing her one. She took it. Her knuckles were white against the stem. She ran her tongue over her lips as Finn clinked his glass against hers. Their eyes met.

Izzy raised her glass to her lips—and drained it in one swallow. "I—I'm sorry. I . . . wasn't thinking. I don't usually drink wine."

"No problem." He quickly poured her another.

"I shouldn't." But she drank that one, too. Then she smiled rather giddily and batted her lashes at him.

Finn sucked air. "I think . . . we'd better eat."

He lit the candles, put on some soft music and dished up the meal. Izzy drank more wine and, with her eyes, followed every move he made.

The tremor was back in his hands again. It was the longest—and the shortest—meal he'd ever had in his life. Long because he knew what he wanted to do after. Short because he wasn't at all sure she'd agree.

And if she didn't—if she turned her back on him, if just once she said Sam's name—he knew he'd have to walk away.

He told himself that over and over. Still, he didn't know if he could.

He barely touched his meal. She barely touched hers.

"You don't like my cooking?" he said with a wry smile as she pushed a carrot slice around her plate.

"I'm, um, not very hungry."

"I am." It was bold and stark—a statement of need with no finesse at all. He was beyond finesse as his eyes met hers. He felt the heat rising in his blood. Through the flicker of the candlelight, he thought he could see an equal heat in her. She ran her tongue over her lips once, then again.

"Finn, I—"

He stood up and held out his hand. "Please."

She knew what he was asking. She *had* to know.

She nodded and stood slowly, her eyes never leaving his as she reached out her own hand and lay it in his. He drew her to him, ran his fingers up her arms, slipping the shawl away from her shoulders as he did so. It fell, unnoticed, to the floor.

They stood, bodies barely touching, looking deeply into one another's eyes. And then, slowly, deliberately, Finn bent his head.

He'd kissed her before. It had knocked him for a loop. He was prepared this time—at least he'd thought he was.

But the pure sweet singing that shot through him when his lips touched hers and they opened for him rocked him to the depths of his being. He didn't know how long it lasted—a minute, an hour—it wasn't long enough. He wanted more. He wanted her. His hands slid up her back to hold her gently against him so that she could feel his response.

He lifted his head. "Come to me," he said, his voice unsteady. He looked from her toward the darkened bedroom.

There was a second's hesitation. Then, "Yes," Izzy said.

CHAPTER TEN

SHE loved him.

There was no other reason for doing what she was about to do. No logic. No common sense.

Only love.

Izzy knew, even as she took his hand and followed him into the bedroom, that he was making no promises. She knew he never would.

Maybe, knowing that, she was wrong to give herself that night. But if she was wrong, she would live with it—and with the memory. She needed to share that love just once with him.

She would have that, at least. The memory of loving Finn, of sharing herself with him, body and soul. And if she only got his body, however briefly, in return, well . . . it was more than she'd had before.

She'd supposed from the moment she discovered that they were alone in his friend's house, that seduction was what was on Finn's mind.

He wanted her—she knew that. At least he was circumspect enough not to try to take her when the girls were anywhere around. He was kind enough, gentleman enough, too, not to push even when they were alone.

"Come to me," he'd said. And if it wasn't precisely a question, neither was it a demand. It was a wish—a wish she shared.

And so she went to him.

She stood silently by the bed in the room lit only by moonlight, and savored the slow heat of his touch. She tipped her face up when his hands framed it, and permitted herself to relish the soft brush of his thumbs across her cheekbones, the light pressure of his fingers beneath her ears. She met his gaze unblinkingly, memorizing the hunger in his eyes as he lowered his head and his lips touched hers.

His tongue traced the line of her mouth, parting her lips, tasting, teasing, and Izzy felt herself tremble under the magic of his touch. A flame began to burn inside her, a flame fanned by his touch, by the heat of his breath against her lips. It grew, consuming her, like nothing she'd ever felt before.

And when his hands slipped behind her to ease down the zip on her little black dress, she was glad to feel the night air cool her heated flesh as the dress slid to the floor. Finn bent his head, his hair brushing against her cheek as he pressed kisses on her shoulders, first one, then the other. Then he ducked lower and she felt his mouth on her bare breasts. A shudder ran through her.

"Cold?" He slid his arms under her and lifted her, laying her gently on the bed. He stripped off his shirt and jeans, then stretched out next to her, his arms around her. His skin was as hot as hers. Cold had ceased to exist. She rubbed against him, relishing the feel of his hair-roughened thigh against hers.

Finn groaned. "I almost went mad holding you every night. Not having you."

"You did?" She tried to pull back to look into his eyes so she could tell if he was joking.

"What do you think?" he said raggedly. "Why do you think I have these dark circles under my eyes?"

"That's why?" She was amazed. She smiled and slid her arms around him. "Maybe you should try catching up on some sleep now."

"Yeah, sure." He nuzzled against her, then slid one hard thigh across her legs, pressing against her so that she could feel the extent of his arousal. "I'll rest later. Now I've got better things to do."

Indeed he did. With his hands and his lips he caressed her, bringing every inch of her alive with wanting. He eased himself down to the bottom of the bed to begin with her toes, touching them lightly, tracing a line along the sole of her foot, then kissing each toe in turn.

Izzy squirmed. He kissed her calves, her knees, front and back, the insides of her thighs. Her breath came ever more quickly. She reached for him, taking a fistful of hair and tugging on it.

"Finn! Stop!"

He lifted his head and she let go of his hair. She could feel the cool tingle where his lips had just kissed her thigh.

"Stop?" He looked at her.

"Yes. No. I don't know!" She shook her head, anguished. "I've never—"

He smiled. "I know." There was a note of satisfaction in his voice. "Relax, Izzy. Let me show you how it can be. Trust me."

Trust him? He was going to break her heart.

How could she trust him?

How could she not?

How could she turn away from him now, sit up and reach for her dress and put it back on, pretending that nothing had happened? She couldn't. She needed this. She needed *him*.

Slowly her hands uncurled and she nodded her acquiescence. Finn bent his head again and kissed her knee. Then he hooked his fingers inside the waistband of her panties and tugged them down her legs. She sucked in her breath as he tossed them aside, then slid his hands again to the juncture of her thighs. His fingertips brushed the curls there. Izzy bit her lip.

"No fair," she said, her voice as shaky as her feelings.

He glanced up from beneath a fringe of dark hair that fell across his eyes. "What's not fair?"

"I'm not touching you." She felt like a wanton. She'd never imagined saying such a thing.

"You want to touch me?"

She swallowed. "Yes."

He moved up between her legs. His fingers still brushed against the core of her. "Feel free."

Izzy raised herself on her elbows, considering her options. It seemed somehow just a little too blatant to do what he had done, to simply take hold of the waistband of his boxer shorts and peel them down his hips. She reached out tentatively, touching the sides of his legs with her fingers. Then slowly, carefully almost, she slid them up the front of his thighs. When she reached the leg opening of his shorts, she hesitated for a split second, then kept right on going. Her fingers found him.

Finn sucked in his breath.

"Am I...hurting?"

He shook his head. "It's good. Too good." He stopped touching her long enough to strip his shorts off and cast them aside. There was enough moonlight that Izzy simply stared in wonder at the proud jut of his masculinity.

"Oh, my," she breathed.

Finn gave a shaky laugh. "Oh, my?"

She looked at him, embarrassed. "I'm not used to seeing men naked. You're very...interesting." She measured him with her hand, letting her fingers caress the length of him.

"Izzy!"

She looked up, startled. "What?"

He laughed again and stretched out on top of her. "Nothing. Everything. Here. Let me." And then he was touching her again, his fingers, his whole body working a magic on her that made her ache with longing.

"Oh, Finn! Please!"

He was poised over her now. She looked up at him, the planes of his face silvery in the moonlight, the skin taut across his cheekbones, his expression intent.

"Come to me," she whispered, echoing the words with which he had brought her to this room, this place.

"Yes." The word hissed from his lips as slowly, with exquisite care, he came to her, *into* her.

She felt the sharp stab of pain and tensed. She couldn't help herself.

"I'm sorry—I—" He bit off an exhalation of breath. "Oh God, Iz, you're so beautiful."

She felt a tremor run through him as he pulled back, then slid home once more, filling her. And she reached her hands up to draw him in more fully, to erase any space at all between them. The ache, the need, grew, intensified. She tightened her heels against the backs of his thighs, then surged forward to meet the thrust of his body.

The world shattered around her at the same time Finn shattered within her, her name on his lips. And then he collapsed in her arms, his head buried against her shoulder as he shuddered with his release.

Izzy felt like a butterfly, emerging warm and wet from a cocoon to a new being, a new life. She felt both weak and stronger than she'd ever been, fragmented and more wholly herself than she'd felt in her entire life.

So this was love. Real love. The deep, abiding love of a woman for a man. Timeless. Elemental. Not like the love she'd felt for Sam. Nothing at all.

A sob shook her. She couldn't help it, couldn't stop it. The emotion simply overpowered her.

He *must* feel it, too. He had to. Surely he couldn't have shared such intimacy with her unless he loved her the way she loved him. *Oh, God, thank you, thank you.* And then she was shaken by another sob.

On top of her Finn went completely still. He almost seemed to stop breathing. Only the hard fast beat of his heart against hers and the sudden tension of his body pressing her into the mattress reassured her.

Then slowly, carefully, he pulled back, looking down at her. She let her hands fall and she folded them across her breasts. He looked at them, then up again at her, his expression dark and grave.

Izzy gulped, then sniffled and lifted her left hand to wipe the tears from her cheek, feeling a fool. She gave him a watery smile.

His jaw was locked, his expression shuttered. He muttered something indecipherable under his breath. Izzy frowned.

Then he said, "I'm sorry."

Sorry? He was sorry?

Izzy stared at him, stricken, but he averted his gaze, pulling back, not slowly at all now, almost fumbling in his haste to get away from her. His movements were jerky as he stood up, then reached down and snagged his clothes from the floor.

Izzy didn't move. Couldn't. She simply watched, feeling something akin to horror welling up inside her.

How could he be sorry? But he was. He'd said so. The words echoed over and over in her head. *I love you,* she wanted to shout at him. *I'm not sorry.*

She couldn't say a word.

He'd pulled on his jeans and was buttoning his shirt by the time she found the ability to move. He tossed her panties and her dress at her, not once looking her way as he started toward the door.

"You can shower if you want," he said, jerking his head toward the bathroom. "I'll do... the washing up."

What was she then? Dessert? Izzy sat on the bed, shaking, clutching her basic black dress against her breasts.

Take a shower? Wash away the remnants of their lovemaking?

Lovemaking? There was a laugh. A bitter half laugh, half sob caught in her throat.

She was a fool, all right.

She'd have the memory of this night with Finn just as she'd thought she wanted. But she'd had no idea how bad—or how quickly—it was going to hurt.

It would have been a night to remember—loving Izzy— if it wasn't a night he desperately wanted to forget.

Finn's head pounded and his gut twisted with remorse as he drove back down the mountainside to the hotel. Beside him Izzy sat motionless—and clearly miserable. She hadn't said a word since they'd made love. She'd only sobbed.

Sobbed. Because she'd betrayed Sam.

And it was his fault, damn it.

Finn knew he shouldn't have tempted her. He'd had no right. None. She was engaged—*in love*—with someone else. And in his arrogance he'd done his best— and succeeded—in getting her to betray her fiancé and go to bed with him.

What a guy. You really have a lot to be proud of, he told himself bitterly. In fact he'd never been so ashamed in his entire life. And his ridiculous apology—*I'm sorry, for God's sake!*—didn't bear thinking about.

He dared to slant her a glance now. Her skin was colorless in the moonlight, her cheeks bleached of all that wonderful peachy tone that was so much a part of who Izzy was. Inside was she as changed as well?

No doubt.

And it was all his fault.

He felt sick. Sick and remorseful and contrite. Aware that he'd ruined the best thing that had ever happened to him. Why in heaven's name hadn't he simply told her how he felt, confessed that he'd fallen in love with her and—

Fallen in love with her?

His hands started to shake so hard he had to grip the steering wheel like a vise to control them. Fallen in love with her? Was that what he had done?

He took a careful breath, then concentrated on drawing it in slowly, holding it, and releasing it equally slowly while he considered the notion.

Love itself had always baffled him. He'd never known it—not the way other people seemed to. Of course, they'd had experience with it. He remembered being abandoned, not loved. And if he loved Meg, it was more of a duty than anything else. The same sort of duty he'd shouldered when she'd dumped the girls on him, though he was learning from them about a different kind of love.

It was Izzy, now that he thought about it, who'd helped him learn a different way of loving them. It was Izzy, who hadn't had any duty at all, and yet who had willingly given herself to caring for them who had shown him the generosity of real love—love that was a joy, not simply a burden.

And how had he repaid her?

By making her betray the man she loved. By taking her virginity, her innocence. And God knew—and Finn knew—that he, of all people, had no right to that.

And giving her what in return? His sordid empty self.

He wasn't surprised she had nothing to say even as he pulled up in front of the hotel.

"I'll go park. You go on in." He didn't expect her to wait.

She didn't. She got out and walked into the hotel, not once looking back. He watched her safely in, then found a parking spot for the car.

As he got out, he stared up into the clear, cloudless night. The heavens were vast enough to make a man feel very small and insignificant in the course of the universe—as if what he did or didn't do wouldn't matter at all.

He wished to God that was true. He knew in his heart it wasn't. What he'd done tonight had mattered a great deal. He had destroyed relationships tonight—his and Izzy's, for certain. Perhaps even hers and Sam's.

And for what? For love?

He wished to God Izzy would believe him if he told her that.

She didn't see him when she left. She gave Rorie a sheaf of instructions and a state-of-the-art pep talk about her responsibilities toward the girls. She gave the girls instructions, too, and a state-of-the-art pep talk about how proud she was of them and how she expected them to show Rorie just how wonderful they were.

They said, "Don't go! You're not going, are you, Izzy? Not really!"

But Izzy had no choice.

"I'll write to you," she promised, brushing a hand over their coppery curls.

"But—"

"I will. I love you," she told them.

"But...what about Uncle Finn?" they wailed.

I love him, too, Izzy thought. But she didn't say that. There was no future in loving Finn when he didn't love her—and a world of pain in staying around any longer now that she knew it.

He was sorry he'd loved her. What else was there to say?

She gave each of the girls a hug and a kiss, then she went down the stairs and didn't look back. In her mind, even though she desperately wanted to, she couldn't seem to turn away.

She had a ticket on a late-afternoon flight to San Francisco. First she stopped to see Sam.

He was working, so at least she didn't have to confront him in his apartment. But interrupting him at his office wasn't much easier. Still, his secretary greeted her cheerfully enough and sent her right in.

He looked up and grinned and Izzy felt like pond scum, hating herself for what she was about to do.

"Sam." She knotted her fingers together and tried to keep her voice from trembling.

He stood and came around the desk and she knew he was going to put his arms around her. She backed up, wishing she dared dart around and put the desk between them once again.

"Oh, Sam!" So much for trying to keep her voice steady. She sounded like a banshee, and, oh heavens, those weren't tears, were they? The ultimate disgrace! She swiped at her cheeks desperately. "I'm sorry!" she gabbled. "So sorry. I didn't mean it to happen! I didn't *want* it to!"

He did put his arms around her then, and she gave up and watered his shirtfront with her tears. He patted her back, making soothing noises, and she remembered him holding her like this when her grandfather had died. He didn't say anything until she finally managed to get herself under control, ruining, no doubt, every bit of the makeup she'd so carefully put on this morning. So much for Finn's makeover!

"It's not that bad, is it?" Sam chided gently once she'd stopped sobbing all over the front of him.

"Worse," she gulped. "I can't...can't marry you." She tried to look at him, but she couldn't bring herself to do it. Not, at least, until he touched her chin with his fingers and tipped her face up so that she had no choice.

Warm brown eyes looked down at her with deep concern. "You can't?" There was nothing censorious in his voice. He sounded kind, gentle. Exactly the sort of man she wanted to marry! Damn it!

She started to cry again.

"Why not? You don't have a...communicable disease, do you?" he asked her tentatively after a moment.

Izzy shook her head and sniffed. "N-no. Nothing like that. Or not exactly," she corrected herself. "Sometimes it feels like it," she muttered.

"What feels like it?"

"Being...in love with Finn."

There, she'd said it. As she did so, she twisted her head away so she wouldn't have to look at him then. She didn't want to see the censure in Sam's eyes.

"In love with Finn." He repeated the words softly and with a certain inevitability.

She shook her head desperately. "I don't want to be!" she said, her voice rising in desperation. "It's the last thing I want, believe me! I'd rather marry you!"

"But you can't." His voice was soft and even, still not censorious, just kind of sad. He pulled out a handkerchief and mopped her face with it. "You look like a raccoon," he told her, a corner of his mouth quirking.

"I feel like a weasel. I never meant—"

"I know that. I understand." He kept mopping.

"You do?"

He nodded slowly. "I'm not blind, you know. I could see it that day out at East Hampton. Among others," he added after a moment.

"Then?" Izzy was aghast.

"Before then. The way you looked at him." He shrugged. "You devoured him."

"I never—"

"Well, you sure never looked at me that way."

Izzy ducked her head, embarrassed, knowing full well it was true, hating herself for having been so transparent to him when she was still lying to herself. "I'm a fool," she said sadly.

"No. You're human." He stuffed the handkerchief into her hand. "Here. Hang onto this. You might need it."

"I will need it," she admitted. "I'll probably cry all the way home."

"You're going home? But I thought—"

Izzy shook her head. "The feeling isn't mutual."

"The devouring wasn't one-sided."

"Yes, well, let's just say, devouring and loving aren't the same thing."

Sam's jaw tightened and he gave her a gentle squeeze. "Then he's the one who's the fool."

Izzy didn't know about that. It was simply a part of who he was. But she couldn't explain to Sam the way Finn felt about loving people or about the experience he'd had of family life. It wasn't her place or Sam's business. She gave a light shrug.

He seemed to accept that. "So you're going home to try to get over him?"

She nodded.

"You wouldn't consider staying here? I wouldn't pressure you."

"I can't. I wish I could, Sam. I do love you, just not the way..."

"I know." He sighed. "I think I've always known. It was too easy. Too good to be true. The rapport we felt from the very beginning, like we'd always known each other..."

"Like brother and sister." Then Izzy's eyes widened when she realized what she'd said.

"Exactly. Like brother and sister." He smiled wryly as she slipped off her engagement ring and tucked it into the palm of his hand. His fingers closed over it. "I love you, too, Izzy," he said softly, then dropped a gentle kiss on her cheek. "You'll be a hard act to follow."

Izzy hiccupped. "Hardly." She took another swipe at her eyes with his handkerchief, then she lifted her gaze to meet his and even managed a smile. "You're the best friend a girl could have, Sam."

A ghost of a grin flickered across his mouth. "I think they call that damning with faint praise."

"Hell and damnation!" Finn kicked the film canister across the studio floor and slammed his hand against the cabinet.

Strong didn't even look up.

He supposed he couldn't blame her. She was probably shell-shocked. He'd been ranting and raving and swearing ever since he'd come back from Wyoming five days before. He'd been banging and slamming his way through the office all afternoon. It was almost five-thirty now, and he was sure Strong was counting the seconds until he put her out of her misery and let her go home.

There was no getting away from his own misery. Neither at home nor in the studio. Once he had been able to find refuge in his work. No more.

Maybe it was because all his work for the first three days back was sorting through the film he'd taken in Jackson Hole. Or the film the girls had taken.

It had seemed like a great idea at the time, equipping them with cameras and turning them loose to shoot things from their perspective. He hadn't considered how much of their perspective included Izzy.

He'd snuck enough shots of her on his own. He was expecting to face them. He wasn't expecting all the ones Tansy and Pansy had taken. They had taken dozens— many good ones of the elk in the meadow, long shots of Mount Moran, close-ups of their faces with moose decals stuck to their cheeks—and scores more of lakes, rivers, mountains, boats and hiking trails—all of which seemed to contain Izzy.

Gareth, a misguided romantic if ever there was one, had even blown up a giggling Izzy to sixteen by twenty inches and had hung her on the studio wall.

"It captures her perfectly," Strong had said to Finn that first morning, the one on which he had left the apartment fearing she'd be gone when he came back. "Don't you just love it?"

It tore his heart out.

He'd spent the rest of the day making prints—and seeing more of Izzy—aching to call home and talk to her, to convince her not to go to Sam.

When he got home, she was gone.

"She was in sort of a rush," the new nanny, Rorie, was apologizing nervously. "But she said you'd understand and she gave me lots of instructions."

Finn understood, all right. He managed a grunt. It was all he was capable of. His fingers tightened on the doorknob, strangling it.

"But if you want me to do anything any particular way," Rorie went on quickly, "you just tell me. After all," she added cheerfully, "you're the boss."

"Yeah." Some boss. He looked up at the sound of footsteps on the stairs. Tansy and Pansy appeared, looking at him, distraught.

"Izzy left!"

"She's gone, Uncle Finn!"

And they flew at him, tears streaming down their faces. They flung themselves into his arms and Finn scooped them up, catching Rorie's helpless look as he did. She felt helpless? How the hell did she think he felt?

"Damn it," he muttered, burying his face in their carroty curls. "Oh, damn."

He'd said it a lot more during the following five days. And he felt as helpless now as he had then.

The phone rang and Strong answered it, then held it out to him. "Your sister," she said.

"Hi, Finn! How's things?" Meg sounded on top of the world. She didn't even let him reply, just went right on. "We had a marvelous time, Roger and I. You were absolutely right. We needed to spend that time together— to get to know each other really, really well. And now that we have, we're more in love than ever."

"Great," he said tonelessly.

"We actually got married, just like I hoped we would." She sounded almost amazed. "And now we're back." Her voice rose as she said the words—a prelude, apparently.

Finn hadn't realized that it was possible to feel sicker than he already was.

"We had a simply wonderful honeymoon," Meg went on cheerily. "Just the two of us in a little grass hut on a tiny island near Bora Bora. So quaint and completely beautiful. Awesome. You'd love it."

Finn didn't say a word. Strong was looking at him sympathetically.

"The girls would have loved it, too," Meg rabbited on. "How are the girls?"

"Fine," Finn said through clenched teeth.

There was a tiny hesitation in her voice now. "You aren't mad at me, are you, Finn darling? For sending them to you that way? I knew you'd take good care of them. You and Izzy." He could hear the smug smile in her voice. He wanted to throttle her. "It was so much better than taking them with me." She gave a happy little laugh.

Finn wondered if she could feel the heat of his anger through the phone wire.

There was another pause, then she said, "I want to talk to you about that." Her voice was more serious all of a sudden.

Finn exploded. "You're not getting them back!"

"Not—"

"You gave them to me! You signed them over, like they were parcels. Well, they're not. They're kids. *My* kids! I don't know if it's legal, what you did, but it damned sure is binding. They're mine, Meg. I love them a damn sight more than you do and they love me. I'll make it legal. You try to take them back and, I don't care if you're my sister, I'll fight you in every damned court in the land! Understand?"

Strong applauded silently and gave him a thumb's-up sign.

"Goodness." Meg took a shaky breath and gave a little nervous laugh. "You always were the passionate one, weren't you?"

Was he? Apparently he was.

"Well, I'm certainly glad I was right," she said. "Don't worry, darling. And you don't need to be quite so testy. I wasn't going to take them back."

Finn's brows drew down. "You're weren't?"

"I simply wanted to be sure all was well."

"It's fine." If you didn't count the crying before bedtime over missing Izzy even yet. If you didn't count the nightmares and sad faces around the breakfast table, the We Want Izzy poster campaign that Pansy had launched, and the "You can make her come back, Uncle Finn," insistence that Tansy wouldn't give up on.

"Good." Meg gave a satisfied sigh. "Maybe Roger and I will fly out and see you in the next month or so."

"You'll be disrupting things if you come that early. Give us some time."

"You're probably right," his sister said. "You do need to bond." She giggled. "I bet it's a kick, watching you and Izzy and those girls."

It was a kick, all right. A kick in the gut.

"Izzy's gone," Finn said flatly.

"What?"

"She's gone. What'd you think?" he demanded. "That she'd throw over Sam Fletcher to stay with me and a couple of kids? Don't be an idiot."

"She didn't?" Meg said in a small, bewildered voice.

Finn said a very rude word. Strong's eyes widened; she pursed her lips.

"But I thought she would," Meg continued in that same small voice. "I don't understand why she didn't. You're perfect for each other. Any idiot can see that. Even you," she added almost as an afterthought.

"I did see it, damn it!" Finn came close to yelling at her. "*She* didn't."

"I don't believe that," Meg said bluntly. "She's miles more perceptive than you are." Her voice took on a suspicious tone. "Did you drive her away, Finn MacCauley?"

He didn't answer her.

"I swear, Finn, sometimes I despair of you. You didn't think I'd leave the girls just to you, did you?"

Finn bristled. "What's wrong with me?"

"You're short-tempered, irascible and stubborn, for starters," Meg said frankly. "But—" she cut him off when he started to speak "—you're also loving and caring and you'd do anything for the people who matter to you."

"Thanks," he said grimly. "I think."

"You would. And I'd do anything for you. That's why I sent you Izzy—so you'd have someone to love like I have Roger. Someone who'd love you, too."

He couldn't believe she was so naive. On second thought, maybe he could. "Izzy doesn't love me. She loves Sam Fletcher, damn it."

There was a long silence. Then, "Does she?" Meg said quietly. "Are you sure?"

Lots of people left their hearts in San Francisco. Not Izzy. All the rest of Izzy's body had been back in San Francisco for a week. She'd left her heart in New York City.

But she was trying to make the best of it, trading jokes with Digger, framing pictures with Hewey's help, watching soaps with Pops, trying to smile and pretend that, even without her heart, she was going to be fine.

"That damn Sam Fletcher," Hewey muttered, running a mat knife down the edge of a swirling black mat. He and Izzy sat in her basement shop, working side by side.

Or rather Hewey worked. Izzy couldn't seem to keep two thoughts together, except when they had to do with Finn.

"Gordon must be spinnin' in his grave. Thought we could trust 'im, your Sam. I'd like to run 'im through." The knife flashed wickedly in his hand.

"It wasn't Sam's fault," Izzy said quickly. She hadn't explained when she got back. She'd just come, smiling wanly, letting them think what they wanted. But she knew she couldn't let them continue to blame Sam. "It was mine, Hewey. I was the one who broke the engagement."

"I thought you loved him."

"I thought so, too," Izzy murmured, bending her head over the picture she was backing.

"Then...how come you reckoned you didn't?" Hewey had apparently decided he'd been circumspect long enough. Now he was getting to the bottom of Izzy's reddened eyes and blotchy face even if it meant asking her point-blank what had happened. Maybe that was just as well. Maybe she needed to face it point-blank—and then move on.

Izzy nibbled on her lower lip, trying to decide how to explain. "Were you ever in love, Hewey?"

"Scads o' times." He gave her his best sailor's leer.

She smiled. "No, I mean *really* in love."

"Heart-stoppin' like?" He regarded her through rheumy blue eyes.

Izzy nodded and watched as a sort of faraway smile lit his face for a moment, making her wonder what—or who—he was seeing. But then his smile faded and he seemed to come back to earth with a thud.

"Just once," Hewey said. "But she was engaged to someone else so I had to let her go." He sighed and ran a hand through his thinning white hair. "Hell of a thing. I shoulda fought for her, but I was too damn noble."

"I'm not." This voice was harsh and so entirely unexpected that Izzy was glad she wasn't holding the mat knife; she'd have cut her hand off.

She jerked her gaze up to see Finn standing at the foot of the stairs. He looked exhausted, worn to the bone, as if he hadn't had a good night's sleep in a week. Exactly the way she felt. She stared at him, poleaxed. Hewey looked from one to the other of them, his curiosity obvious.

"Not what?" Izzy said faintly when she at last could speak.

"Noble. Apparently." Finn's mouth twisted. "I tried. Didn't work. So then I went around to knock Sam's block off."

Hewey's jaw dropped.

Izzy swallowed carefully, wanting to blink, but not daring to, even for an instant. She was that afraid he might disappear. She ran her tongue over her lips, then made herself concentrate on breathing. It was more difficult than she might have thought.

"Why would you want to...knock Sam's block off?" Was that her voice, that tiny, pathetic sound?

"For having you." Finn said it flatly, but she saw the way his fists clenched at his sides and his knuckles turned white.

"He doesn't."

"I know that. Now." His voice was harsh. "He told me you'd broken off your damned engagement a week ago. A week!" He glared at her.

She nodded. She didn't know what else to do. She wished Hewey would close his mouth. She wished he'd put down that mat knife. She wished he'd go upstairs!

"You the reason she's been mopin' around like a brigbound sailor?" Hewey asked, fixing Finn with a hard stare.

Finn's jaw tightened. He looked as if he might tell Hewey exactly where to get off with his interference, but apparently a second's reflection made him think better of it. "Was she?" His voice held a hopeful note.

"Damned right," Hewey said. "Poutin' around here like somebody shot her fav'rite dog."

Finn didn't look certain whether he ought to be pleased by that comparison or not, and Izzy didn't know, either. She wanted to know what he was doing here! Why, against all odds, he'd come! A thousand half-born hopes rose in her heart, but she needed it spelled out.

"Hewey," she said, "I wonder if you'd mind going upstairs."

"What for?"

She raised her eyebrows at him, then looked at Finn.

"Oh," Hewey said, comprehending. He shoved himself up off his stool, then hesitated and looked back at her. "You reckon that's what Gordon would do?"

Obviously he saw himself as *in loco Gordonis* since her grandfather's death.

"Yes." No. Her grandfather would have asked a lot more interfering personal questions than Hewey, but at the moment she had enough of her own.

Hewey looked Finn up and down, then apparently decided to reserve judgment. He headed for the door. "Reckon I'll just take this here mat knife with me." He flashed it—and a deadly smile—at Finn as he passed.

Neither of them moved until Hewey's footsteps sounded in the hall upstairs. "I found out Izzy's problem," Izzy heard him shout to Digger.

"I know. I let him in," Digger replied.

"Don't mind them," Izzy said, forcing herself to look back at Finn.

"They're the least of my problems." He shoved a hand through his hair, took a step toward her, then stopped. His blue eyes bored into hers. "I didn't even try to be noble," he said in a low voice, "until it was too late."

Izzy looked at him, perplexed. "What do you mean?"

"If I'd been noble I wouldn't have made love with you in the first place. I wouldn't have taken you up to George's and seduced you. I'd have been like your friend there—" he glanced up the steps.

"Hewey," Izzy supplied.

"Yeah. Noble to the core. And lonely as hell. I didn't want that. So I played dirty. I wanted you to want me, not Sam." His voice dropped. "But you didn't."

Izzy waited a heartbeat. "I didn't?"

"You started crying, for God's sake! We made love and you burst into tears!"

"Because I thought it was only sex to you, that love had nothing to do with it," Izzy told him.

"*What?*" He stared at her. "*That's* why you were crying? Not because I'd ruined you for Sam?"

"You'd already done that."

He scowled. "What do you mean?"

She drew a deep breath and met his blue gaze head-on. "I thought I loved him...until I met you." She had nothing to lose.

He looked stunned. "You...love...me?" He sounded as if he was speaking a foreign language. Maybe, Izzy decided, given his past, he was. Maybe that night had been as hard for him as it had for her.

She found courage in that idea and moved toward him, stopping just inches away. "I wanted the memory," she confessed. "I thought it was all I'd ever have."

"Oh, God." The words seemed to strangle him. He loosed his fists and took her hands in his. She could feel the tremor in them as they gripped hers. "Oh, God, Izzy. I do love you!"

He kissed her then, long and hard and with all the need he'd been storing up for Izzy couldn't even guess how many years. Finn might have given other women his body, but she knew without a doubt that she was the first to ever get his heart.

The tears started again. She thought they were hers, but when he wiped his eyes, too, she wasn't sure. She laughed shakily and so did he.

"How did you know I was here?" she asked him.

"Sam told me."

"Sam?" Had he done that for her, too?

"He wasn't exactly surprised to see me," Finn said wryly, "when I finally lost the rest of my nobility and found enough of my courage to beat his door down last night. In fact he said it was about time."

Izzy smiled. "Dear Sam."

"I wouldn't go quite that far," Finn said darkly. "If it weren't for Sam I'd have had you a lot sooner."

"If it weren't for Sam, you wouldn't have me at all. I was coming back to New York for him."

"Maybe," Finn allowed. "And then there was Meg. She set us up."

"What?" Izzy stared at him, astonished.

The skin across his cheekbones reddened slightly. "She reckoned we were perfect for each other. That's why she sent the girls with you."

"She knew I was engaged to Sam!"

"Yes, well, you know Meg and scruples. She doesn't have many." He grinned.

Izzy made a harrumphing sound, but she couldn't really get angry at Finn's sister. Not when for once Meg had actually been right. "She's wicked," she muttered.

"Thank God," Finn said, clasping his hands behind her back and bringing their bodies together. "Otherwise I wouldn't have you—or the twins." He shot a fleeting glance up the steps again where Izzy could now hear, along with Pops and Digger and Hewey, the sound of Tansy and Pansy giggling.

"It nearly killed them when you left," Finn said quietly.

"It nearly killed me to leave. But I couldn't stay, not when I thought—"

"I know." Finn's lips touched hers. "But now you're staying. Forever." He hesitated, a worried flicker in his eyes. "Aren't you?"

"If you want me," Izzy said.

"Yes," Finn said. "Oh, yes, I want you. I want to marry you. I want to have children with you."

"More children?"

"If you don't mind," Finn said quickly. "But we are keeping Tansy and Pansy. I told Meg that." He grinned. "We can go on a honeymoon to Bora Bora. All four of us."

All four of them. Izzy laughed and put her arms around him. "Sounds wonderful. Shall we go upstairs and give them the news?"

"You think they'll like it? All of them? Even the old man with the knife?" He sounded just a little apprehensive.

Izzy hugged him. "Don't worry. I'll save you."

He kissed her once more, a promise of loving yet to come. "You already have, Izzy my love. You already have."

HARLEQUIN PRESENTS®

Don't miss these fun-filled romances that feature
fantastic men who *eventually* make fabulous fathers.
Ready or not...

Watch for:
June 1997—FINN'S TWINS! (#1890)
by Anne McAllister
July 1997—THE DADDY DEAL (#1897)
by Kathleen O'Brien

FROM HERE TO PATERNITY—
men who find their way to fatherhood
by fair means, by foul, or even by default!

Available wherever Harlequin books are sold.

And the Winner Is... You!

...when you pick up these great titles
from our new promotion at your
favorite retail outlet this June!

Diana Palmer
The Case of the Mesmerizing Boss

Betty Neels
The Convenient Wife

Annette Broadrick
Irresistible

Emma Darcy
A Wedding to Remember

Rachel Lee
Lost Warriors

Marie Ferrarella
Father Goose

Look us up on-line at: http://www.romance.net

ATWI397-R